# WILD
# POPPIES

# WILD POPPIES

## Haya Saleh

*Translated by*
**Marcia Lynx Qualey**

LQ

LEVINE QUERIDO

MONTCLAIR | AMSTERDAM | HOBOKEN

This is an Em Querido book
Published by Levine Querido

Although set during the very real and devastating Syrian war,
locations and characters in WILD POPPIES are fictional.

LEVINE QUERIDO

www.levinequerido.com • info@levinequerido.com

Levine Querido is distributed by Chronicle Books

Library of Congress Control Number: 2022945147

ISBN 9781646142019

Printed in India by Replika Press Pvt. Ltd.

Published June 2023
First Printing

*We are condemned to hope. The things that are happening today cannot be the end of history.*

—Saadallah Wannous

# PART ONE

## Omar

# Chapter One

R unnnnn."
    "Runnnnnnnn!"

I startled awake to my sister's screams. I reached over and slipped an arm around her, pulling Thoraya's head up against my chest. The threads of early dawn light made it just bright enough for me to see the terrified look in her eyes.

"We're safe here; don't be scared," I said, trying to comfort her. "Nothing's going to happen to you here. I promise!"

Our mother jolted awake, too, and she called for Thoraya to come sleep on her lap. She kissed her and made her arm into a pillow for Thoraya's head. Then she started to sing to my sister, the way she used to before the war:

> *Sleep, my little one, oh sleep,*
> *Lord, I pray her soul to keep,*
> *Oh, I'll cover my baby up so tight,*
> *Oh please, God of Mercy and Might.*

My family all lived together in one small room. It was the one that had been assigned to us by my mother's aunt Sajida, in her house in the country. There were three other rooms that were filled up with relatives who had fled the ruins of their cities and villages. Like us, they had come looking for safety, far from the places where the fighting raged.

Our aunt's house was in a village called Al-Nuaman, which means "the poppy flower," and it's called that because wild poppies grow here in the spring. Every year the hills and valleys around the village look like young women wearing holiday dresses. All of them are covered in bright flowers, and the wheat fields stretch out in all directions.

The biggest room in our aunt's house was for her eldest son and his wife, and the second was for our cousin and his wife. In the third, another cousin lived with her husband, plus her husband's parents. But there were no big get-togethers between the owner of the house and all these guests. Everybody stuck to their own rooms and barely came out, because every family was too busy taking care of their own basic needs for food, water, and medicine to worry about anyone else. Maybe they'd managed to escape the war. But what they hadn't realized was that the war's fires would keep on burning them up, even from afar.

All the noise that Mama and Thoraya were making woke up my little brother Sufyan. He got up off his mattress and walked over to Thoraya, who's six, and said, "Open your hand. I've got something that will make you into a brave girl."

Thoraya opened her tiny palm, and Sufyan dropped a small, black beetle into it. He jumped back when Thoraya shrieked in terror, and my mother's voice rose thunderously as she shouted curses at him.

Sufyan is the only one who can still upset Mama and make her lose her temper. Ever since our dad was martyred and our house destroyed, she's been transformed into a totally different person—someone who seems strong and stoic and calm. She hardly ever shouts at us, like she used to before. Instead, she's usually silent, maybe because her head is filled up with the sounds of bullets and explosions, and that drowns out everything else.

Sufyan left the room, and things calmed down. Mama went back to singing to Thoraya, and a gentle breeze slipped through the window. I sat down against the wall and pulled my knees up against my chest. As our mother's soft voice slid over me, it reminded me of how she used to sing so quietly to me when I was little, and it took me back in time.

Before the war, we had a house in the peaceful city of Raqqun. There, we'd walk back home from school in total safety, with no bullets and no bombs. And, when my dad got back from a different school, where he taught physics, Mama would have our lunch ready. I can still smell the mouthwatering dishes she cooked and baked: molokhia with chicken and rice, or kibbeh, or mansaf with lamb. After lunch, I would go with Sufyan to play soccer in our neighborhood, or else I'd go out with my friends and walk around in the souk, or maybe I'd go with my dad to the farm that he had inherited from my grandfather. There, I'd help him pull up the weeds, or prune back the almond trees, or cut the grapes off our vines. I thought we would live our whole lives like that: happy, loving, and in peace. But then one single siren announcing the outbreak of war was enough to end it all. Even though only a few months had passed since that siren, it felt like it had been more than a hundred years.

But I remember the night when the bombing started. Baba woke us all up, sweaty and terrified. His head was bare, and he was wearing only a flannel shirt and pajama pants. He shut all the windows tight and turned off the lights. When the bombing got heavier, and we could hear people screaming, we ran out toward the big State Hospital. By then, hundreds of families had run out of their houses, looking for somewhere safe. There were women, old people, children—some had run away from the rain of fire coming down from the sky, and some were running from the bullets that flew out from behind the buildings, fired by people we couldn't see. Some had died and become martyrs.

Our dad tried to protect us from the bombing by sheltering us with his own body. He held us in his arms, and we felt safe like that, because those two strong arms had never once failed to protect us, and they had never once let us down.

The shelling got heavier, and the gunfire got closer and closer. People were running in every direction. I glanced up at the sky, and it looked like it was lit up red and orange with lava. Then I couldn't see Baba anymore. I turned around, looking for him, and found him standing unsteadily right behind me. He'd been hit by shrapnel. Baba waved his right hand at us, motioning to us to turn away and keep going, while holding his left hand clamped against the side of his body. Blood was gushing out; his hands and clothes were soaked in it. I tried to run toward him, to save him. I wanted to stay by his side. But a young man who was nearby grabbed me and dragged me away as I kicked and punched at the air.

I screamed as hard as I could: "Baba! Baba! Baba!" and then I lost consciousness. When I woke up, sadness hung over the world, and soldiers like living ghosts crowded every part of the city.

Before the bombing, sometimes I'd hear Baba talking about what he thought might happen if war broke out in our country. He would talk about it on the phone, or else in the evenings at the café, as he sat around with his friends. He'd say that other countries would kill us from the skies while our own internal conflicts would kill us from the ground. Back then, his words didn't mean anything to me. I was sure that this "war" he was talking about would happen somewhere else, and that it couldn't possibly reach *us*.

On that first day of fighting, the voices of crying children, weeping mothers, and old people sobbing were all mixed up together. For the first time, I smelled the stench of blood. I couldn't stand it, and I kept on throwing up. The whole place was covered in rubble, and the rubble filled up my chest, more and more, until I could barely breathe.

# Chapter Two

It was just before dawn when Thoraya finally fell asleep.
Mama nodded at the empty water jugs. "Omar, habibi,
you need to go out early to get water. We nearly died of
thirst yesterday." I got up out of bed—the August heat
dragged me down like a pile of heavy blankets. I picked
up two plastic jugs and headed out toward the yard of
the nearby refugee camp, where they handed out supplies of pasta, rice, lentils, and water. Qattoush, Sufyan's
dog, was standing at the door and panting from the heat,
and he followed me. I looked around for Sufyan, but I
couldn't find him.

I pushed aside the tires that surrounded the house so I
could get out, and Qattoush walked through the safe
zone along with me. Ever since Sufyan had decided to
keep and raise him, this dog had never stopped following me around, trying to get closer to me.

We'd found Qattoush when we started collecting tires
to build a fence around our aunt's house. Before that, our

houses had never really needed walls to protect them—the state of peace we had lived in was protection enough.

When we were carrying the tires, we found tiny Qattoush hiding inside one of them. He was a half-starved little puppy with a cut on his left ear. He must have been chased by bigger dogs and discovered that the tire was a good hiding spot, and that he was safe in there. Even though I pitied the poor thing, I refused to let Sufyan keep him, since Mama has diabetes, and we need to keep all germs and dirt away from her, because she has a weak immune system, and we don't want her health to get any worse than it already is. But Sufyan insisted, and Mama was sympathetic, so I gave in to the idea—on one condition: that the dog must never, ever come into the house. And so the deal was sealed.

Now, Qattoush circled me and rubbed up against my pant leg to express his thanks. I petted his head to express my gratitude, too. It had taken me a while to start confiding in Qattoush, sharing all my secrets, and I found all my talking didn't bother him. He was full of life and joy, and loved to play. I'd throw him an empty plastic container, and he would chase after it until he caught it, and then he'd bring it back to me. As the days passed, he got to be friends with the other kids in the village. He even made friends with Rakan, who everybody knew was a bully and a troublemaker who mocked and beat up the other kids, snatching away anything of theirs that he wanted.

Finally, I got to the camp, and I filled up the two jugs. God alone knows how much pollution there was in this water. Just by looking at the murky brownish color, you could tell it wasn't fit for drinking—let alone if you got a whiff of its musty smell or took a sip, since it tasted like the inside of a rusty drainpipe. But what could we do? There was no other choice.

I picked up the two jugs and went to stand in the long line to get our rations. As usual, there was no set time when they would arrive, which made the waiting even harder. Qattoush stretched out by my feet while I watched the girls in the yard playing the hat game. It's this game where everyone sits in a circle, and one of the kids has a hat. The kid who has the hat walks around the circle, and they have to drop it behind someone—then *that* kid chases them around the circle. Each of the kids was looking around at Salma as she walked slowly and hesitantly past them.

"The green hat," Salma sang.

The other children sang back: "What's inside it?"

"Green raisins."

They chanted: "Give it to us."

"And the fox . . . pass, pass, pass . . . his tail takes seven laps . . ."

Then she threw the hat at one of them, and they all laughed.

I watched them, trying to force myself to wait more patiently. Then I heard Thoraya call out to me, and I could hear her panting from a ways off. By the time I turned all the way around, she was standing in front of me. "This is from Mama," she said, holding out a small sack with two tomatoes and two small, round loaves of bread.

She tossed me the bag and ran off toward the girls, so she could play with them. I noticed Sufyan was on the other side of the open yard, playing marbles with his friends. I called out to him, and he waved back at me. Qattoush saw him and darted off, racing toward Sufyan. The pup's tongue flew out and he spun around and around in circles, as if he were chasing his own tail, and he didn't cut it out until Sufyan ordered him to stop.

Qattoush immediately followed Sufyan's command, which was the opposite of what he did with me. He was afraid of Sufyan, just like our little sister Thoraya. Even Sufyan's friends went out of their way to avoid making him mad. Otherwise, how could you explain the way he always won at marbles? Sufyan was twelve, and he was already solidly built. He was clever and observant, but he was impulsive and moody, too, and so I had to be extra sure to watch him, to make sure he didn't get in fights with the other boys.

He had a strong personality, and that had always been the excuse I'd given for refusing to take care of him, which had irritated our father. Sufyan never listened to me, no matter what I tried. Even though I was the oldest,

Baba could tell I wasn't capable of taking care of my brother and sister, or of looking out for Mama, either. Even though he didn't say it out loud, I understood it clearly from the way he looked at me. Still, at the time, it didn't really bother me. I was convinced that my family wanted nothing to do with me, and that the more I stayed away from all their annoyances, the more I'd avoid problems and punishments. Plus, most important, I was sure that Baba wouldn't leave us, and that he would take care of me and our family forever.

When Baba passed away, I discovered that there is no such thing as the word *forever*. Since then, I've been doing my best to protect Mama and Thoraya, and I've been trying even harder to protect Sufyan, even though sometimes I feel helpless when I remember all the things I *can't* protect them from, like this cursed war and all its weapons of destruction. Bombs are hurled down at us from the sky, while an army of monsters is destroying everything on the ground.

Sufyan has always been hard for me to handle. Once, he asked me to hit a boy who had beaten him up on his way home from school. Sufyan's shirt had been ripped, and dirt had been ground into a gash in his cheek. He was furious at me when all I did was stop the other boy and talk with him, calmly—especially when I told the two of them to reach out and shake hands and forget what had happened. Sufyan's face twisted up with rage before he grabbed a handful of dirt and threw it at me, and then he ran back to the house and wouldn't speak to me for days.

I was shaken out of my memories by a woman's voice saying, "Ooooof. May God have mercy."

She had been sitting on the ground in front of me, waiting. All the people who had been in line since dawn's first light had started to get restless. It seemed like maybe the supplies wouldn't come at all today, and that would mean more days of hunger. I saw Abu Safwan, one of the camp managers, walking toward us. He had taken a liking to me, since he'd been a friend of my father's.

He lifted a bullhorn up to his mouth and announced that the supply trucks headed for the refugee camps had come under fire. We were used to this sort of news. Sometimes, the trucks got bombed. Sometimes, they were stopped at a checkpoint. And sometimes, the armed militias of different opposition fighters took the supplies for themselves, or else they were looted by gangs of thugs.

I heaved up my water jugs and started to walk home. Sufyan followed me, and Thoraya trailed after him.

Thoraya tried to help me carry the big jug in her two small arms, saying, "They won't come today, right?"

I didn't want my answer to be without hope, so I said, "They'll come tomorrow, inshallah."

I glanced over at Sufyan's face. He had remained silent, his expression joyless. He knew that supplies wouldn't come any time soon, and maybe they'd never come at all. He was full of anger and resentment because, like all us refugees here, he knew the meaning of hunger— the kind of hunger that made you feel like your guts were so empty, they might start devouring themselves. He kicked a pebble with the toe of his shoe. As it shot off, he said nothing.

Mama was waiting for us in the house's front yard, and when she looked at my hands and realized I hadn't gotten anything, she swallowed the dry words that were stuck in her throat. Then she said, with a forced smile, "No problem. We'll find some wheat and rice."

I knew she was just saying that to force us to be a little patient. War had taught us to be good at tricking everyone, even ourselves. And when Thoraya started to grumble and complain about being hungry, Mama discovered that those two pieces of bread and two tomatoes had been the last food we'd had.

"I'll eat anything," Thoraya said. "Anything, even if it's a piece of plastic."

"Have a little patience," Mama said sympathetically. "I'll look around the house, and maybe I'll find something to cook."

I wondered how Mama would find something in a house that was so crowded with hungry mouths. It was a place where, whenever anyone got a bite of food, they would hide it from the eyes of all the cousins and uncles and aunts living in the house until they got to their own room and ate it with their own family. But before Mama stood up, I saw Salma heading toward us, carrying a black bag. She smiled and waved while giving me a shy look.

"Hello, Salma. It's good to see you." Mama welcomed her, and maybe part of this welcome was directed at what Salma was carrying.

"This flour is from Mama," Salma said, sitting down on a rock near me. In the summer sun, her mix of brown and blond hair glowed. Her bronzed face shone, too, and her eyes were an even brighter green than usual.

Our mother's eyes gleamed, too, as she looked at her little treasure, and then she picked up the flour and hurried off to prepare the dough, while I got up to kindle the fire we cooked on. We used a wood fire because of the sky-high price of gas, and plus all the power outages. Salma ruffled Qattoush's fur and kept looking at me, as though she was urging me to say something, but I was too busy collecting the firewood and building the fire. After a few minutes, Thoraya tugged on Salma's hand, wanting to play with her.

Salma was a nice girl. She was thirteen, with a skinny body and gentle features that hid her strength and intelligence. I knew that she had a soft spot for me. Her eyes followed me whenever I passed by, and she would squirrel away a few of the delicious things her father brought home so she could share them with me: a piece of chocolate, a can of soda, a bottle of clean, clear water. Her dad had been a big-time merchant before the war, and after it started, he had come to the village of Al-Nuaman looking for a safe refuge, renting a house near Auntie Sajida's.

Mama came out carrying a bowl full of batter for bread. She put the iron skillet on the fire and flapped at the hot smoldering logs with the edge of her pink-and-purple flower-print scarf. Then she poured the batter into the pan, and after a while it started to smell of fresh-baked bread. We ate bread with tea, and, even if it wasn't the most delicious or satisfying meal, it was enough to take the edge off our hunger. Mama hid the rest of the pieces for us to eat that night, setting aside one round loaf of flatbread for Auntie Sajida and another for Sufyan, who had disappeared and didn't share in our feast.

The smell of fresh bread reminded me of the times I used to go to the bakery with Baba. When I was little, he would take my small hand in his big, rough one. But after I started school, he would let go of my hand and force me to walk alone, and he even made me cross the street alone.

Two days ago, I dreamed about my dad: I was walking down a dirt road that was filled with sharp stones, and I saw him walking toward me. He opened his arms for me, and I ran toward him, ignoring the painful stones that were stabbing into the bottoms of my bare feet. But before I could get to him, a wall of fog rose up from the ground and stopped me from reaching his arms. From a little ways off, I heard his confident voice: "Don't be afraid, you can cross it. Come on, you're a man now."

I tried with all my strength to get through the fog. But when I finally made it, I looked around for my dad and couldn't find him.

When I woke up, I realized it was just a dream. I searched the dusty shelves for the book *The Interpretation of Dreams,* but I couldn't find it, even though I was sure I had seen it there before. Instead, the book *The Hunchback of Notre-Dame* fell into my hands, and I flipped through and decided to read it, putting it down only after I'd turned the last page. Then I took a deep breath. It was as if a hand had gently pulled me out of my world and set me down in another one. Ever since we had left our house, I had stopped reading books the way I used to . . .

Ohhh, I missed my books so *much!*

That night, we were all really anxious, since Sufyan hadn't come back. I took Qattoush and went out looking for him, but we couldn't find him anywhere. I went to the nearby refugee camp and started racing around the tents like crazy, and Abu Safwan even picked up the bullhorn and started calling out for Sufyan, but we got no answer. I went to the oak tree where he sometimes played with his friends, but no one was there.

I panicked. By the middle of the night, everyone in the village was searching along with me. I climbed up a tall cypress tree and looked all around, hoping to see my brother, even though it was pitch dark and you could barely see past your own fingers. At that moment, I thought about how we might really lose Sufyan forever, and I shouted in a panic: "Sufyaaan! Sufyaaaaan! Sufyaaaaaaaaan!"

# Chapter Three

"He'll be back soon. Don't worry." Salma's voice rose up to me from beneath the branches.

I hurriedly climbed down, but before I could bombard her with questions, Qattoush started to bark as he dashed toward the turnoff for our village. We ran after him, and there—in the distance—we saw Sufyan. It felt like a dream, and I rubbed my eyes and looked at him, and then I rubbed my eyes again in disbelief.

I had meant to scold him and shout at him and give him a forceful shove when he came back, but now I forgot about all that, and I threw my arms around him without thinking, and I cried and cried. I cried all the tears that I'd stored up, ever since Baba had passed away. I cried from the pain . . . I cried from the happiness . . . I cried from the fear.

"Did you know where he'd gone?" I asked Salma.

"N-not exactly," she stammered.

My voice was louder than I meant it to be. "If you knew something, then why didn't you tell me sooner?"

"He made me swear not to breathe a word about it," Salma said, and then she ran off, crying.

Only a few minutes passed before people started to crowd over and check on Sufyan. He told them that he'd gone out in search of food, but then he'd gotten lost on his way back. He said he couldn't figure out which road would take him back to the village until it was very late.

After his explanation, people went back to their homes and tents, and I sat down with Sufyan in the yard in front of the house, around the embers that flared up and went out, off and on. My heart had almost stopped worrying about Sufyan, and it was now glowing with happy gratitude for his safe return. Mama joined us, placing a pot of water with steeping herbs on the embers.

She shifted her sitting position, and then said, "We were out of our minds with fear, Sufyan. Tell us what happened. I want to know every single detail."

Even when Mama said that, Sufyan didn't show any sign of regret, and he didn't say a single word of apology. He got up, took a bundle out of his pocket, and tossed it into Mama's lap. Both of us watched his face.

"I went back to our house in Raqqun," he said.

Mama gasped, and then she clapped a hand over her mouth. "Crazy," she said. "There's nothing left there for us to go back for—unless you want us to die of grief for you."

"I've been thinking about going back to our house to get my savings for a long time. So I borrowed a little money from Salma, and I went. I took a car until I got to the first checkpoint, and after that I walked. It was easy enough to recognize our house, since it wasn't totally destroyed—not like Umm Saad's house, or like our neighbor Asaad's, or the rest of the houses in the neighborhood. Except the stairs were wrecked, so I climbed over the piles of rocks and searched my room until I found my money."

"You put your life at risk for the sake of a piggy bank?" I asked. "Have you lost your mind? We're in the middle of a war."

His eyes flicked between me and our mother. "You've got to believe me, the road really was safe. All the houses were either destroyed or deserted, and everyone I met at the checkpoints was nice and let me through. Nobody did anything bad to me."

My mind was busy trying to fill in the blanks Sufyan had left in his story, since he was the type who wouldn't tell you the whole thing. To test him out, I asked, "What else did you bring back from the house, besides your money?"

He reached under his shirt and took out my notebook—the one where I used to jot down quotes I liked from whichever book I was reading. He opened it up and took out a family photo that had been hanging in the living room.

I remembered the photo so clearly. We had taken it one Eid al-Fitr, because my dad had bought a new camera, and he had wanted the first picture to be one of our family. We had all gathered around him; I was ten at the time, and Sufyan had been in second grade. Mama was standing next to my dad, holding Thoraya, who wasn't even a year old yet. My dad had asked my uncle Mansour, who had been the first person to visit us that Eid, to take the picture.

He'd told us, cheerfully, to say, "*Chhheeeeeeez!*" and we'd all laughed at the burst of the camera's flash. Uncle Mansour was also martyred in the war.

Mama didn't seem excited to see the picture. Her mouth was still set in a straight line, and she just said in a firm voice, "This time you were safe, okay. But you can't go back again. Understood?" Then, without waiting for a reply, she went inside.

That night, I watched Sufyan's face as he fell into a deep sleep, and I still felt there was a missing link in his story. Something wasn't right. I didn't know what it was, exactly, but it sat like a heavy weight on my chest.

In the morning, Salma came over. She was wearing a long, pink dress and she'd tied back her soft, smooth hair in a white bow. She didn't come up to the front door, but instead she sat on the tires and started petting Qattoush. When she saw me walk out, she stood up, rearranging her dress and nervously pushing back her hair.

She spoke first. "I'm so, so sorry. You have to believe me, I was just so focused on helping Sufyan."

I turned my face away from her. "But you hid it from us. Sufyan's still just a kid. Didn't you think that your money might take him to his death?"

"No," she said. "I didn't think like that. He told me his uncle would come get him, and then he'd bring him back right away."

"And you believed him??"

"I'm sorry, but I did. It's the truth, I swear it." She looked at me with tears welling up in her eyes.

"I believe you," I said, trying to make her feel better. "But please never do that again. Promise?"

"Promise," she said, smiling kindly and wiping at her eyes with a palm.

Mama looked out the window and called to me. Salma excused herself, and I climbed up the stairs to our room. Mama stood next to Sufyan's bag, which was sitting open on the table. The paper money was missing—after she had counted it last night, more than once.

"It has to be Sufyan who took it," I said calmly. "It's not possible that a thief came in while we were sleeping. Plus, a thief would have stolen all the money and left nothing behind, so that we couldn't accuse anyone."

"You're right," she said. "But why didn't he tell us? That boy is going to drive me crazy."

Just then, Auntie Sajida knocked on the door of our room and stepped in, saying that she'd seen Sufyan leave shortly after dawn. When she'd asked him where he was going, he had told her that he was rehearsing a play with his friends.

In the past, Sufyan used to be really good at memorizing lines and imitating voices, and he was especially good at reciting poetry from old-fashioned plays. Whenever someone came to visit my dad, the guest would call for Sufyan and ask him to perform some scene, and Sufyan would stand there and improvise confidently. When he was finished, he'd bow, and all of us would applaud.

# Chapter Four

Mama urged me to go look for Sufyan, so I went out right away. It didn't take long to find him, since he and his friends were all under the oak tree, building a rough platform from planks of wood. I even saw Qattoush carrying a small piece of wood in his mouth, as if he were trying to help.

"Sufyan, what are you doing?"

When he answered, his voice came from between clenched teeth. "Welcome, Omar. We're building a theater."

"A *theater*?" I said, dumbstruck.

"Yes," he said, hammering a nail into the wood. "We've decided that we're going to put on some cool shows. And whoever wants to see them has to pay in cash."

I walked up to him, took the hammer out of his hand, and looked him right in the eye.

"Why didn't you tell me? How could you just take the money like that?"

"Well, if I had told you or Mama," he said indifferently, "then you wouldn't have let me do it."

"All right then," I said. "How about you return the wood and those carpentry tools to their owners and get your money back?"

"Believe me," he said, stubbornly returning to his work. "We're going to make a ton of money doing this."

"People here don't have enough money to buy food, so where are they going to find the cash to pay to watch your ridiculous little shows?"

That set him off, and he said fiercely, "You're always against me! Okay, so you don't want to do anything to help us. I mean, you're afraid to even *think* about doing anything to help the family. So why don't you just let me do it?"

"I'm not against you," I said firmly. "But it's my job to protect you."

"You're not my father, who can tell me what to do. Baba's not here anymore."

"That's why I'm responsible for you since Baba died," I said, taking his hand and pulling him away.

He struggled, shouting at me: "Let go of me! I'm old enough, and I know what I'm doing."

"No," I said, holding on tight. "You're going to come with me."

"I hate you," he shouted, trying to wrench his hand free. "I hate you!"

After a few struggling steps, we stopped. I didn't leave until he agreed that he would return all the carpentry tools and get his money back. But later, I found out that he'd coated all the wood in black pitch, so the owner wouldn't let him return it. When I told Mama and our aunt what Sufyan had done, they didn't get angry. Instead, they laughed. And because I'd wanted to see Mama laugh again so much, I laughed along with them— it was a sound that I'd hidden away somewhere deep in my belly.

When Mama spoke, her voice was full of tender affection. "Sufyan's always going to be a troublemaker, and that will never change."

The next morning, Sufyan and his friends didn't miss a single house as they went from door to door, trying to sell bits of scrap paper that they called "tickets" to their first-ever theatrical performance. But they couldn't sell a single one. And so Sufyan took apart the platform and carried the wood to our yard, with some help from his friends, so that it could be used as firewood.

The weird thing was that he didn't seem to feel any guilt or regret about his failure. Instead, he told me he was thinking about *another* project that would make him some money. And when I asked him what it was, he said he was going to open a convenience store!

"He's a tough one, like your father," Mama said, when I told her what he'd said. She added: "When he's relaxed, you'll think it's impossible to ever make him angry. And when he's angry, you'll think it's impossible to ever calm him down. He's strong and stubborn, and he doesn't forget when someone does him wrong, not even once in years and years."

I nodded. I'd known my father too. He used to say, "People who are generous deserve our forgiveness, but those who are mean-spirited don't deserve anything at all."

Once, we came across a man who was around Baba's age in the big central market. When he walked up to us, I saw he had a long scar that went from his forehead all the way down to the top of his chin—and his face got stamped on my memory. The man stretched out a hand and said, "Hello, old neighbor." But Baba didn't greet him back or reach out a hand to shake his. Instead, he pushed me in front of him, and we hurriedly walked away. I asked my father who this man was, and Baba said he used to live near us in Raqqun before he left the neighborhood a few years back. He said that Asaad— that was the man's name—was a thug who made a lot of problems, and that he'd attacked shops and forced their owners to give him payouts. Baba said this man spent his days going around with a bad group, that he hung around the streets and preyed on the weak.

"This man is a demon who wears the cloak of an angel," Baba said. "Like lots of people, I had an unfortunate confrontation with this *sultan*, when he and his thugs wanted to take money from me and some of our neighbors. But we stood our ground and fought back, and so they hit us with canes and batons, knocked us down, kicked us in the stomach. After that, I made a complaint to the police, and he was sent to prison. There, he fought with one of the other prisoners, and that's how he got that scar on his face. After he came out, he was still furious with me, and he wanted to get his revenge. But I stopped him, filing another complaint with the police, and they forced him to sign a pledge never to hurt me again."

"But why is he saying hello to you now?" I asked. "Maybe he could have changed?"

"Mm," my father said. "I heard that, overnight, he became the imam of a mosque, and now he teaches people religion. But I doubt he could know a single thing about that." He added, sarcastically, "He changed his name to Sheikh Abu al-Bara."

With the money that was left from Sufyan's piggy bank, we had enough to buy a few supplies. Of course, our priorities were lentils, bulgur, flour, and a few fresh vegetables. In the last few weeks, prices had gone up again, faster than we could have imagined. A few men were hoarding things, and then they charged huge amounts for basic foods, since they knew that—during a war—people didn't have any other choices. They were squeezing even the emptiest of pockets, while they had more money than they could ever need. Parents watched their children die of starvation and disease, ashamed by their helplessness. I used to believe there was one kind of death, where the soul would leave the body. But here I had seen lots of kinds of death, and plenty of bodies without souls, even though the people in those bodies were still alive.

Again and again, the bombings and thugs stopped the supply trucks from getting through, sometimes for a long time, so that people ran out of patience. Their faces were sickly pale, and things got even worse when sickness broke out because of all the pollution in the water. Plus, there were shortages of medicine, and the doctors' clinics were doing less and less. Because of all this, Mama's health got worse and worse, until she could barely get around anymore. Even though she tried to seem strong and to hold it together, we could feel her silent pain as she hid the swelling in her feet, and we knew she was having a hard time breathing, even though she tried to keep it from us. She'd turn away so we wouldn't see her grimace. Eventually we could see that she was feeling sick all the time.

One night, I woke up to the sound of Mama coughing so hard it sounded like she was going to retch up her intestines. I jumped up and started looking around for her, and I found her sitting on a tire outside, as if she didn't want anyone else to hear even one of her moans.

"Mama," I called out to her. "Are you okay?"

She didn't say anything, and I hurried up to her. But before I could grab the hand that was reaching out toward me, she fell to the ground.

# Chapter Five

The doctor on duty at the clinic examined my mother, and then he did a bunch of tests. Afterwards, he took me aside and told me that she had to rest and take her medicine on a regular schedule so that she wouldn't develop kidney failure. Mama waited at the clinic while I took the prescription and went to the public health center's pharmacy. But the things he'd prescribed, like most of the things that doctors prescribed, weren't available. I stopped in at a few private pharmacies and asked how much the medicine would cost, and the number shocked me! I realized there was no way I could get her medicine, since I didn't have even a single bill in my pocket.

Mama had diabetes, I knew that. But she'd never had a history of kidney problems!

When I went back and told the doctor that I didn't think Mama had kidney problems, he told me that diabetes can lead to kidney disease. I begged him to help me out, but he just shook his head sadly and went in to see another patient. I walked helplessly back to my mother, who was still lying on the examination table. I helped her up, and we left. When we got to the clinic's front door, I folded up the doctor's prescription and tucked it into my pocket, since I couldn't do anything more with it right now anyway.

I was as weak as a paper boat, as lonely as a single nail hammered into the wall. I spent most of that day sitting on an overturned bucket in the yard, obsessing over how useless I was. The little kids were racing around the neighborhood like they usually did. I watched them when they came near me: half-naked, their hair shaggy and stiff from all the dirt caked on them, their feet bare and cracked. Still, they found time to play, as if feeling the bright sun on their faces and playing a silly game was all that mattered.

I smiled as they made a circle and chanted: "It's your turn! The sugar bowl . . . fell out of my hands . . . and cracked and rolled."

The older boys were playing soccer. Rakan and his friends had made a ball by stuffing an old sock full of torn-up bits of fabric. They were counting all the goals they made against the other team, but they refused to count any of the goals the other team made against them. And if anyone protested, they would threaten him, and then that kid would stay silent out of fear that they'd beat him up.

My mind had turned into a camera that captured all the things around me, even the parched ground, the empty juice containers tumbling by, and the defeated looks on the adults' faces. It recorded everything, beyond even what you could only see in a moment, storing up people's voices, their movements, their features. Ever since we had left our home in Raqqun, I'd been trying to resist the images that shoved their way into my mind day and night. But even if I survived the war—even if a hundred years went past—I didn't think I could ever forget how we had to run away from our home, and the cruelty of this miserable life that me and my family were living right now.

I saw Sufyan walking toward me, a hand shoved down into his pocket. He stumbled as usual, since of course his shoelaces weren't tied. It annoyed me that he still hadn't learned how, even though I'd put a lot of effort into teaching him, step by step. He stood in front of me and took a few bills out of his pocket. They were crumpled up from his tight grip.

He said, without even saying hi or anything, "Omar, take this and buy the medicine for Mama."

"Where did you get it?" I asked.

"I sold my marbles."

I looked down at the money he'd put in my hand and saw that it wasn't enough to buy even one box of the medicine the doctor had prescribed. I moved over so he could sit down on the bucket, and we shared the narrow space.

Then I twisted around so I could look him in the eye. "Thank you, Sufyan. But you should have told me before you sold your toys. If you had said something, I would've told you not to do it, since we need a lot more than this to buy Mama's medicine."

"Keep the money," he said, his face still open and vulnerable. "I don't know, maybe somebody like my friend Salma might be able to help us get the rest of it. And that way, we'd have enough for Mama's treatment."

"Yeah, absolutely," I said. "I'll hang onto it."

He stood up, so I bent down to tie his shoelaces. When he walked away, he said a soft goodbye and gave me a grateful look.

A little while later, I saw Salma handing out sweets to the other kids. I thought about Sufyan's suggestion, and I decided I would ask her father to give me a loan, which I would pay back after everything calmed down. Even after the bombs had set off fires in his warehouses, devouring all his goods, he kept doing business. Except now it was through barter. People traded whatever electronics and appliances they had been able to carry off with them when they escaped their homes in exchange for lentils, rice, flour, and whatever else he brought from the city.

While I was still thinking it over, Salma ran up to me, saying, "Hi, Omar." Before I could respond, she put some money in my hand, which she'd taken out of her pocket. She mumbled, "This is to buy medicine. Take it."

"But how did you know I needed it?"

"Everyone knows your mother needs medicine," she said, not looking at me. "Please take it."

I didn't want to pester Salma with a lot of questions, since what really mattered right then was finding a way to get the money for Mama's medicine, because that was her lifeline. I thanked Salma. And even though I felt really, really grateful, I was ashamed, too, since I'd never accepted someone's charity before.

I watched Salma as she walked away, the pink skirt of her dress floating around her in the breeze. Then I took in a deep breath and looked up, trying to calm down all the chaos of my thoughts. I wanted to feel as clear as the sky, which was sharp and blue with no birds anywhere.

I remembered the roof of our house in Raqqun, and how I would stand up there and watch the flocks of pigeons flapping through the sky. And I remembered my pellet gun too . . .

Baba had bought a pellet gun for me, and one for Sufyan, on one of the Eid holidays. We had spent every minute playing with them, prowling around and hunting anything that stuck out in the house, until Mama had enough of it and almost snapped the guns in two. The next day, Baba took us on a family trip to the Barshun

Mountains, where he'd been born. He *loved* to hunt. It was a passion that he'd inherited from my grandfather, who had inherited it from his father before him. So it was a family tradition. Baba slung his rifle over his shoulder, and Sufyan and I carried our plastic guns.

Mama would always grumble when we'd go off mountain climbing, but Baba would say, "You must teach your children swimming, archery, and horseback riding." She would shoot back, laughingly: "Archery?! And exactly what century are you living in, my dear husband?" At that, we'd all be gasping with laughter.

I tried to avoid any creature that moved, even the insects. Our hunting trips terrified me, although being with Baba made me feel a bit safer. He used to say, while he carefully watched the game, "Hunting is a sport of intelligence, played out between the hunter and his prey. Only those with speed and quick wits can win." I watched him freeze in place so he wouldn't make a sound, since animals would notice even tiny things, like a stone being kicked or a branch being snapped. After all, Baba told us, they had a much keener sense of hearing than humans.

My father always reminded us, "You've got to understand the behavior of the animal you're hunting, so you can anticipate its reactions and know what to do next."

Whenever Baba would aim a gun at his prey, I would lift my eyes up toward heaven and secretly pray to God that his bullet would miss its mark. He tried to teach me to hunt, but I refused to even think about carrying a real rifle, much less point it at an animal. After he gave up on me, he went on to teach Sufyan, who wasn't even nine yet. He taught Sufyan how to hold a rifle steady, using the laws of physics that Baba had both studied and taught: "A rifle sets off an equal but opposite reactional force. And if you don't keep it under control while you're shooting, it's going to slam into you, and you'll get hurt."

Sufyan took all this very seriously, and he spent a lot of time practicing. He'd aim the rifle at any far-off target that our father suggested: a stone, an empty juice bottle, or a piece of fruit hanging on a tree branch.

Then Baba would give Sufyan fond looks, with his eyes half-closed, as if he couldn't imagine being any prouder. Once, he handed him the rifle and pointed out a hare in the tall grass. Sufyan's face lit up with a grin, as if he'd been given a gift. He raised the gun and aimed with one eye shut. He waited for the right moment, then shot his hare. Baba's mouth fell open in amazement. After Sufyan had brought back his quarry, he tossed a craggy rock down the path and bet Baba that he could hit it.

And he really did—Sufyan hit it again and again, until he was sure that Baba was convinced of how good he was. When Baba asked him what method he used to hit his target, Sufyan said confidently, "To be honest, it's my own special kind of method. I squeeze my eyes until I see two shadows of the target, one in each eye. Then I aim for the spot right between those two shadows, where the real target is. It's got nothing to do with physics or anything."

Baba laughed and patted his shoulder, saying, "Indeed, I've never heard of anyone doing it quite like that. But the important thing is that you're a skilled hunter, and I'm proud of you."

The next morning, Sufyan and I were standing by the window in our room, each of us playing with our pellet guns. The challenge was to hit any of the apples on our neighbor Asaad's tree. I tried to hit one and failed. But Sufyan managed to hit an apple that fell down and rolled—unfortunately for us—until it landed right at our neighbor's feet. He glared over at our window. It was only a matter of minutes before he was sitting with Baba in the room where our parents received guests.

"Tell your kids not to come anywhere near my tree," Asaad said.

"What did they do?" Baba asked him.

Asaad took the apple out of his pocket and pointed to the place where the pellet had gone in. "Look at this," he said, and Baba stared at the apple. But instead of apologizing to Asaad, he said joyfully, "What a hit! That's amazing."

"Excuse me, but what exactly are you saying? I came here to complain to my neighbor about what his kids have done. And you're, what, happy about it?"

"Forgive me," Baba said. "Of course, I'll warn them that they shouldn't go near your garden, or even the window that looks out on it."

Oh, how I miss my father!

After he died, they didn't wash his body, since the sheikh told us that martyrs aren't washed. I looked down at his face as he lay there. For a moment, I imagined he was sleeping and just pretending to be dead, the way he used to do when I was little. He'd lie there until I fell for it and started kissing him, and then he'd wake up and attack me with hugs and tickles, asking, "Do you love your baba?" and I'd nod, laughing and crying. After they had thrown the dirt over him, I fell down at the edge of his grave, wanting to weep. But the tears had frozen in my eyes.

# Chapter Six

I bought the medicine for Mama, and then, on my way home, I saw Sufyan riding with two of his friends in the back of a dusty, armored jeep. I tried to catch up to them, but the jeep sped off before I could get there. I stood at the turnoff to our village, waiting for Sufyan to come back. I stayed there until sunset, and then I decided to go to our room so that Mama wouldn't worry. But as soon as I reached our door, Sufyan slipped in right behind me.

I tried to breathe slowly, to steady my nerves. Then I grabbed his arm and pulled him out into the yard, so that Mama wouldn't find out what had happened, which would probably make her blood pressure go up or worse.

"Where were you?" I hissed at him.

He stared at the ground, absentmindedly kicking at the dirt with the toe of his shoe. "I was selling tissue packets at the turnoff for our village."

I grabbed his shoulders and glared right into his eyes. "Yeah? Then where's the money you got for them?"

"I lost it." He told this second lie with total confidence.

"You're lying, Sufyan. I saw you."

He wrenched himself out of my grasp and ran to our room, calling for Mama to help him. She stood between us while Thoraya sat in the corner, watching us in silence like a house cat. I told Mama what had happened, and she was so furious that she snatched up her medicine and threw it across the room. Sufyan said that the two men he'd gone off with were good people, and that they helped others, and that they'd driven him to Raqqun when he went to get his piggy bank. After that, they brought him right back here and gave him double what he had in his bank.

"Why didn't you tell us all this before?" I asked him.

"I was afraid you'd get mad."

"That means you know you made a mistake," I said. "That's why you hid it. Right?"

"No," he said, his voice rising. "It's because you get mad at everything I say or do."

Mama cut in, using her gentle voice now, clearly struggling to stay calm. "We love you, Sufyan. We're your family, and we love you. These people kidnap children and traffic them. I'm sure you don't want to risk that happening, either to you or to your friends."

Lately, everyone had been talking about the violent gang crime that was spreading everywhere. These men had started flogging, stoning, kidnapping, imprisoning, torturing, and killing . . . The things they did were worse than a person's mind could comprehend. They were like the stuff of myths and horror stories, except they were even more terrifying.

Mama spent the whole night talking about the dangers of these gangs, which she said were taking advantage of children's naïveté, and about how quickly a child could be convinced to join them. Sufyan refused to listen. The only thing he paid any attention to was how Mama had referred to him as a child. He said that she should know that he was grown up now, and that no one was going to be able to trick him, and that those two men only wanted to help. At that moment, I screamed at him with all my strength, and then I leapt on him and grabbed hold of him, so that he couldn't move his legs or feet. I threatened him, telling him that, next time, I wouldn't just stand by in silence! I saw terror flicker in his eyes, and I let him go only after he swore that he'd stay away from strangers.

I couldn't sleep. I walked out of our room and headed for the living room. The television was blaring news about one of the armed groups, and they showed a picture of a man who the TV news anchor said was a leader in some organization called "the Falcons of Truth." The man's face stuck with me, because it reminded me of that man who had been harassing Baba. I looked at the long scar that ran down the face in the photo, and I would almost swear it was him—except in this photo, he looked different from the man I remembered; thinner, maybe, his gaunt cheeks making him look even meaner.

The next morning, Sufyan woke up and went to wash his face. When Thoraya walked past him, he flicked water at her with his hand, and then made her think that he'd spit the water out of his mouth. "Ew! SUFYAN!" she shouted, before bursting into tears.

I snorted, looking over at Sufyan, who had a devilish twinkle in his expression as he brushed his teeth and sang at the same time, words garbled by toothpaste bubbles. Ahh, I loved him and I worried about him so much! I remembered the way he used to count me in on anything he got. Whenever he bought something at the supermarket with his money, a bag of chips maybe, or a candy bar, he'd get something even bigger for me. And as soon as he got home, he'd run toward me and say in his funny melodramatic way of his, "Oh, my dear Lord Omar, I have brought you a *gift* that you will absolutely *adore*. This chocolate has come from the ruler of India, and these chips from the ruler of Sindh."

"And the ice cream?" I'd ask.

"That, my lord, comes from the distant Persian lands." And we'd fall down laughing together.

It never occurred to me that, after that morning, I would miss Sufyan's face. But one day he left and didn't come back.

# PART TWO

## Sufyan

# Chapter Seven

When Baba died, a lot of things died with him. In the days right after, when I missed him so much, Omar tried to stand by me, his hand on my shoulder. He said he would take Baba's place now, that *he* would protect us . . . Except I knew he couldn't do it, and I didn't understand why he insisted on ordering me around, or why he kept telling Mama what to do. And she kept saying, "Omar's your big brother, and now he's going to take on the role of your father too."

Omar might be a good brother, sure, but he could never replace my father. Baba was always telling him, "You're all grown up now, so act like a man." Because he DIDN'T. And I didn't trust what Omar said or did because he was a weakling and a coward. I felt like *I* was the one responsible for our family after Baba left, not Omar, and I had to do everything myself. The problem was that, every time I did something, Mama and Omar found a million reasons to criticize me, and they never said even a single word of thanks.

Ever since we'd left Raqqun, I had been thinking about my piggy bank, because I'd put a lot of coins and even bills in there, over a whole year, since I was saving up to buy a PlayStation. If it was still under the bed and no one had noticed it, there would be enough money there for us to buy all the stuff we needed. When I told my friend Rayan what I was thinking, he said that, if he were me, he'd go to the house and look for it.

It wasn't a new idea—it had crossed my mind a bunch of times. But I'd always hesitated.

Finally, with Rayan's encouragement, I decided to go back to Raqqun. But how could I get there, when I didn't have even a single coin?? I found the answer when I saw Salma on her way home. She's nice to everybody, *and* she has money. Plus, most important, she needs me so that she can get close to Omar. I know she likes him, since she never stops talking about him—it's always *Omar did this*, and *Omar did that*. And every time we say goodbye, she tells me, "Tell Omar I said hi."

I walked with Salma to the oak tree, where we used to meet. There, the girls played on a swing that they'd made out of an old car tire, and the boys played with marbles. I told her I needed some money. Then I added, looking her straight in the eye, "I'll get it back to you. Soon."

"Your family needs to buy food and stuff," she said. "Right? Does Omar know?"

"Look, my family has nothing to do with this, and Omar doesn't know a thing about it." I said all this calmly, as if I were just stating facts. We kept on talking, and I tried to convince her. "Salma, listen. My uncle's going to come and take me back to our house in Raqqun, to where I hid my piggy bank. I'll get it, and then I'll come right back with my uncle. Everything will be fine."

"What does this uncle of yours do?" she asked.

"He's a distributor," I said confidently. "And since he brings stuff around, he knows all the roads, and I'll be safe with him."

She startled me with her next question. "So then why do you need money, if your uncle's going to take you there and bring you back?"

I wished she would stop asking stuff so I could stop making things up!

"Because it's not my uncle's car; he just rents it. So I have to at least help him out by paying my share."

"Okay," she finally said. "I'll get you the money tonight."

I begged her to keep it a secret, just between us, and she nodded in agreement. But I still didn't feel sure about it, so I asked her to swear.

At my insistence, she grumbled, "I swear to God that this will stay a secret between us."

Early the next morning, I stood waiting at the main street, right after the turnoff to our village, trying to flag down any car going south. A dusty white jeep stopped. There were two men inside: The first one had a big head, a pale face, and a short beard with his mustache shaved off. The second one was even paler, with brown hair, blue eyes, and a long beard.

"Where are you going, my son?" the man with the short beard asked, his voice kindly.

"To Raqqun," I said.

"Get in," the man with the long beard said. "With God's help, we'll get you there."

Their friendly way of talking gave me the nudge I needed to get in. Along the way, I told them my family's whole story, start to finish, and I found out that they worked at a center that taught religion and took care of kids. They said that they gave food, and drinks, and even gifts to the kids who participated in their lessons.

They drove me to my house in Raqqun, waited for me, and then took me back to the turnoff for the village of Al-Nuaman. But before I got out of the jeep, the man with the short beard, whose name was Abu al-Qaqaa, said, "Today's Sunday. We'll expect you on Thursday. Don't forget. The center is in the next village over, in al-Jib. It's not far from here."

The second man, Abu al-Ghazanfar, said, "Bring your friends, too, and your reward will be doubled. It will be a good deed."

Then he gave me a few bills. At first, I hesitated. But they said this was a gift, and I had to accept it so that their reward with God would be doubled. I stuffed it in with the money I'd found in my piggy bank. I couldn't believe it—I had such a huge amount of money now that I could get everything I'd dreamed about. I could buy a Play-Station if I wanted, except that the electricity was always going out, and everybody would be mad at me for buying expensive electronic stuff when people couldn't get enough to eat.

Then I thought about what the two men had offered me: an easy job that would help everybody. It was like the best kind of dream.

# Chapter Eight

I didn't go to the educational center that Thursday, like I'd promised, because Mama was so sick. But I did go the next Thursday, after I'd talked a bunch of the boys who I trusted the most into coming with me. I didn't tell them what would be there—I wanted it to be a surprise.

At the center, they were happy to see us. Abu al-Qaqaa saw us and walked right over, welcoming us and leading us into a big room where there were clean mattresses and pillows laid down in neat rows on the floor. They'd left a space for a chair, which we knew would be for the person responsible for teaching us.

Inside that room, we saw there were other kids already waiting, so we sat down in the empty spots. Then the sheikh came in. He was a kind-looking man with a gray-and-black beard, an all-white ghutra on his head, and square orange glasses. He greeted us and said, "You are the nation's torchbearers and the generation of righteousness."

From the way he talked, he sounded like my old Arabic grammar teacher from before the war, and I found the stuff he said almost impossible to understand. Well, we were bored, but we survived it!

Rayan poked me and whispered, "Are you getting any of this?"

"Doesn't matter," I told him. "I only came to eat."

Quietly, we laughed.

Then the sheikh nodded. Before starting his prayer, he told us, "I will pray, and you all will say *amen.*"

We lifted our palms up, and whenever he finished one of his long cycles of prayer, it was our turn to say, with our eyes half-closed, "Ahhh-meeeen." We were careful to stretch out the *ahhh* and the *eeee* a lot.

Rayan poked me and whispered happily, "Prayer means we're almost at the end of the lesson."

A few minutes later, the sheikh stood up, and we all rushed out of the room. Abu al-Qaqaa called out to me, saying, "May God bless you, Sufyan. You are serving the Lord well." That was the last time I saw him.

They asked us to go into a big room. It was filled with round tables that looked kind of like the dining table at our old house, rubbed smooth with wear. On the middle of each one, there was a big, black pot of bulgur, rice, and meat, plus three big plates of salad with tomatoes, cucumbers, and onions. Each table also had seven bowls of garlicky-smelling red-lentil soup. I looked at that feast with hungry, eager eyes—I hadn't seen anything like it since we'd left Raqqun.

After we'd finished eating, they gave us each a set of gifts, including pellet guns, plastic pistols, marbles, juice boxes, candy, dried fruit, and bags of dates.

The center's leader was a man called Abu al-Harith, who had a wide face, thick eyebrows, and soft hands, and he even put some money in my hand. "The more you work, the more you'll get," he said encouragingly. "Next time, invite more of your friends."

We took our spoils and left, so happy we could hardly believe it was real. Rayan had put some of the leftover food in a bag to feed his family, and he put bones in another bag to feed his cats. He said, in a cheerful voice, "Even my cats are going to celebrate tonight! I hope little Soma's foot is healing up fast. Can you believe the other kids from the camp tried to hunt her down and eat her? But I saved her."

Well, yes, I believed it! Even though killing a cat sounded cruel, hunger was even crueler.

We went back to the village. I decided not to take anything home with me, since Omar would start up his interrogations, as if he was Detective Conan, and Mama would back him up the way she always did. Meanwhile, I'd have to invent fairy tales to fend them off.

I thought the oak tree would be the best place to hide my stuff. I thanked God there was no one there but me.

I dug a hole about twenty feet away from it, between there and the orchards, next to a heap of stones. I named it "the secret stash," and I buried my booty there after I'd put it all in a cloth bag I'd found in our aunt's house and tied up tight.

I guessed that I'd have to dig another pit to fit all my stuff, since I was going to be getting more of it.

I divided up the money I'd gotten into two piles: one was to pay off my debt to Salma, and the other was for Omar, so he could buy the medicine that Mama needed.

As soon as I got back to the room, Omar practically jumped out at me. "Where have you been all morning?"

"I was playing with the other kids," I said, not looking him in the eye.

"Where?"

"By the oak tree."

"That's a lie!" he shouted. "I was there, and I didn't see you."

"Rayan and I *were* playing there," I said. "Then we had a fight with the other kids, and we decided to go somewhere else."

Omar gave me the same suspicious look he always did. So I turned to Mama and gave her my long-suffering face, trying to get her sympathy. "Mamaaaaaaaa, every time I come home, Omar jumps on me with the same old questions. Uffffff."

"He's worried about you," she said.

I turned my back on them and raised my voice, "I don't need anyone to worry about me. I'm not a kid anymore. I've grown up."

I went outside and sat in the yard for a little while, until I calmed down. Then Qattoush and I went over to the oak tree, where I scratched his rough coat. Salma was there, playing on the tire swing, her dress tidy and spotless as always. She waved and said hi.

"Thanks for not telling anybody about the money I borrowed off you," I said. "Even though I told Omar and Mama right away anyway."

"Actually, I told Omar, too. He was worried about you. He really loves you a lot."

"Yeah, yeah. I know."

"He asked me not to help you again," she said.

"I know."

"I promised him I wouldn't do it again," she said, jumping down on off the swing. "So don't be mad at me."

I gave an indifferent shrug. "Wait here, and I'll get you your money back." Then I dropped my voice, even though there was nobody else around. "And I'll tell you a secret, but you'll have to *promise* me you won't tell anyone about it, no matter what, not even if Omar asks you a thousand questions. Otherwise, I'll never trust you again."

"Okay," she said. She looked like she was trying not to smile. "What's the secret?"

I showed Salma my hiding place, and then I dug up the bag carefully, with my hands, and paid her back her money. I asked her to give the rest of it to Omar, so that he could buy the medicine for Mama. But, I told her, she should say it was a present from her. And to stop Salma from hitting me with all her million questions—exactly like Omar and *his* million questions—I hurried to distract her by taking out the pellet gun. But my plan failed, because Salma had already started up her interrogation.

"Sufyan, where did you get this?"

"I've been working," I said.

"You're *working*? Where . . . and with who?"

"I've been selling tissue packets out on the main street, at the turnoff to the village. Sometimes people feel really sorry for me and give me double the price."

"Does Omar know about this?"

"No, and please don't tell him," I said. "I told you because I trust you. I'm working so I can save up enough to keep on buying Mama's medicine. Promise me you'll keep this a secret, just between us."

"Your secrets are endless," she protested.

"This is the last one. Please?"

"Okay," she said, her face serious. "I promise."

I grabbed Salma's hand and pulled her back toward the tree. I climbed up first, and then I helped Salma get up. Qattoush raced around the trunk, barking, and I told him to hush.

"Choose any target, and I'll hit it," I said.

"Any target? Any target at all?"

"Anything," I said.

"Okay, what about that cypress tree?" She pointed to a nearby evergreen that was covered with little, round berries.

"Sure," I said confidently. I aimed my pellet gun at the tree and hit a berry, then a second berry, then a third. The louder Salma clapped and cried out, the bolder I felt.

Then she insisted, "Let me try," so I handed her the rifle.

She shot at nothing, and then she lost her balance and tumbled out of the tree. Qattoush jumped on her and started licking her face. Thank God she wasn't hurt. The whole way back, we didn't stop laughing.

# Chapter Nine

Nights in the village go by so slowly. I'd lie there, on my mattress, and all the old memories would light up inside my head.

I remembered Baba. . . .

I remembered my friends in our old neighborhood. Where had they gone?

I remembered our house in Raqqun, which made me sad, since it had been destroyed, and it would be impossible to build it back the way it had been.

I remembered my room, which was hit in the bombings. My chair—the chair Mama had made from a tree trunk, the one she'd carved my name on in English—had been shattered into pieces. My books and notebooks were burned up, and the pages were scattered everywhere. The wall that Omar, me, and Thoraya had decorated with drawings of Spider-Man had collapsed. I used to dream about becoming a superhero like Spider-Man. It took me a long time to realize that Spider-Man wasn't a real hero. Real heroes—like Baba—helped people without having any magical powers.

I couldn't sleep because there was this giant mosquito that never stopped bothering us, making its annoying high-pitched whine and biting us without mercy. Plus there was a little moth that hovered around the light, taunting me. Plus the sheets were ripped, and they had a smell that reminded me of rotten pickled cauliflower.

I looked at Thoraya, who was falling asleep in Mama's lap. I scooted over to sleep next to her. But the insomnia wouldn't leave me alone, so I tried to distract myself by watching the bulb that was hanging from the ceiling.

"Get away from me," Thoraya grumbled, after I tickled her nose with a piece of straw and woke her up.

"Okay," I said. "Turn off the light and I'll leave you alone." I pointed to the switch on the wall.

She got up and flicked it with her little finger, and the room went dark. I felt annoyed by the darkness, so I said, "Turn it back on." When the light came back on, I made a scary face, and then I laughed and turned it off, then on and off, all while I opened my eyes and mouth wide, sticking out my tongue and giving a stupid look. We didn't stop laughing until Mama raised her voice. "Quit fooling around. I'm tired and need to rest."

Mama's health was getting worse. I didn't really think it was diabetes, like Omar said. I think it was because she was listening to the news. The news in this country is all miserable. And it's the news in this country that's making people sick.

In the morning, I went to the center with a group of boys to continue our lessons. After we finished, they gave us sandwiches, juice boxes, and presents, and Rayan even got an expensive cell phone, since he'd given the right answer when the sheikh had asked us how to punish infidels. Rayan had raised his hand and said, "We'll kill them all."

It was an answer that had never really crossed my mind, and I was so jealous of Rayan that, when Abu al-Harith gave me money, I asked him for more. I had decided I was going to buy *two* phones just like Rayan's, one for me and one for Omar—even though I didn't know how I could give a phone to Omar without him getting suspicious.

After Omar had bought Mama's medicine from the money I'd asked Salma to give him, he had some left over, so Omar had bought Mama a phone, so she could call our other relatives and check in on them. He did it even though I told him not to. After all, the news she'd get from the phone would be even worse than the news she'd get from TV.

I kept going to the center, and I earned enough money to buy lots of the stuff that we needed. I didn't dare give Omar a big amount all at once, since he would launch an investigation and maybe even find out where I was going. So I gave him a little at a time, and each time I would have to make up a good story about where I had gotten it: I'd sold my marbles, or I'd collected empty cans out on the road, or I'd found some copper wiring. I didn't think Omar ever totally believed me, but he still took the money. Because after Mama got so sick, getting her medicine and the other basic things we needed was the only thing he could control.

One day, Abu al-Harith asked us to all gather in a big open yard, and he started having us do military training exercises that he said were necessary if we were going to learn to defend ourselves. We had to do this, he said, because our country was at war. He called out to us, "You are not children. You're men! Heroes! And with these weapons, you can beat back your enemies, and the enemies of God. Then, you will enter Paradise through the widest of all possible gates, where you will find everything you've ever dreamed of."

He waved his machine gun and said, "Say it with me: 'Death to the infidels.'" Then he repeated it. "Say it louder: 'Death to the unbelievers . . . death to the unbelievers.'"

We repeated after him without really understanding what we were saying. And, as the days went by, it became like our group's anthem.

At the center, they started teaching us about stuff I'd never known about before. Like, for example, I didn't know that I shouldn't talk to Salma or even go near her, and that God punished girls for showing their hair or face. I wanted to warn Salma, except how could I, since talking to her was forbidden. So I told Thoraya to tell Salma—except it seemed like my message didn't get through, since Salma didn't cover either her hair or her face!

One day, I got up the courage to ask Mama to cover her face. Her head jerked around, and she looked over at me and asked, "Who taught you that?"

"Nobody," I said. "I learned it from religion class—a looooong time ago. Back at school."

"I'm not going to cover my face," she said lightly, like she didn't even care. "I can barely catch my breath with my face uncovered."

"But the face is a private part," I said anxiously. "I don't want you to go to hell."

"I'm not going to hell, God willing. Do you know why? Because the people who go to hell are the ones who hurt others, and I haven't hurt anyone." Then she looked me right in the eye. "My beloved Sufyan, our religion is a religion of tolerance and moderation. For God, *love* is religion."

In the training sessions, most of the other boys could hardly hold onto a pellet gun while they were shooting. They were even worse than Salma at keeping steady when they took a shot. But Abu al-Harith noticed that I was good at hitting a target, and he asked me to aim at a lot of things: cloth dolls, empty bottles, rocks. . . . And I would always hit my target on the very first try, which made him so happy that he gave me a real gun that was even bigger than Baba's rifle. After a little practice, I could use it like a real professional. Abu al-Harith told us that, next time, we should bring a sleeping bag, because they were going to set up a training camp for us out in the wilderness, and we would only get back to the village in the late afternoon.

That day, when I got home from the center, I didn't do anything important. I just sat in the yard, thinking about stuff, and then Rayan came up holding a real soccer ball. He must have bought it with all the money Abu al-Harith had given him. He asked, panting, "Aren't you coming to play?"

I didn't hesitate. "Yeah."

We got to the field, and—as usual—Rakan was lording over the whole place. As soon as he saw the ball, he said, "That's my ball." The worst part was, all the other boys said, "Yeah, yeah, that's Rakan's ball."

Then Rakan came right up, shoved Rayan in the chest, and snatched the ball away. Rayan jumped on him, kicking and punching, but Rakan just grabbed him and threw him to the ground like a piece of cloth. I tried to hold Rakan back so he wouldn't hurt Rayan—and, at just that moment, I saw Omar striding toward us. That wasn't a comforting sight, since I knew how Omar behaved when things like this happened.

Rakan held onto the ball and turned to Omar. "Go away, coward."

Just as I'd expected, Omar was totally spineless. He went up to Rakan and, instead of cursing at him, he begged him to give the ball back to its rightful owner. Omar kept on trying. "Rakan, please. Give the ball back to Rayan. Stop causing trouble."

Inside my head, a volcano of anger erupted. How could wishy-washy words like this work with Rakan?

Rakan answered in a voice that was a mix of stubbornness, pride, and sarcasm. "The ball's mine, like it or not. Let's see who has the guts to say otherwise."

The boys gathered around us. Omar walked up, cautiously, trying to snatch the ball from Rakan. In one quick movement, Rakan kicked him in the stomach and punched him in the face. Omar fell to the ground, blood oozing from his nose.

Then I had to jump in. I leapt on Rakan, wrestling him down until I got an arm around his neck and my teeth in his ear. He screamed like a baby. He shoved at me with his big, meaty hand, getting me hard in the chest. Then Omar stood up and tried to pull him off me, and the rest of the boys rushed at us. The fight spread, and it got louder and louder, and we didn't stop until Rakan's father showed up. He violently yanked his son up and pushed Rakan in front of him, shoving him all the way back to their house. That was the first time we ever saw Rakan really scared.

On our way home, Omar wiped the blood off his face with the sleeve of his shirt. He said that, when he'd looked into Rakan's angry eyes, all he'd seen in them was fear.

# Chapter Ten

On Wednesday evening, when Mama, Omar, and Thoraya weren't in the room, I took my chance and packed up all my most important stuff in a plastic bag and hid it in an abandoned kitchen cupboard. Nobody would ever think to open one of those cupboards, since they were all completely empty, and the shelves were covered with dust.

Then I went to join the rest of my family in the yard. As soon as Mama saw me, she opened her arms to give me a hug. But I didn't run over and throw myself into her lap like I used to do when I was little. Seriously, I'm not a kid anymore, and they should know that I've grown up.

Mama ran a hand through my hair and sat me down next to her. She studied my face for a long time before she said, "You look so much like him." I knew she meant Baba. I hear that a lot. I didn't react, and she looked from me to Omar to Thoraya, and then she said, "We're a family, and we have to stick together. That way, Baba can rest, knowing he doesn't have to worry about us. We can't let anything separate us."

Even though Mama was saying *we*, I felt like her words were only for me, because she gave a little cough and added, totally unnecessarily, "There are people who manipulate the minds of children and take advantage of them, brainwashing them and filling their heads with evil thoughts, snatching the love from their hearts and sowing cruelty and hatred in its place. And I'm more afraid of those people getting to you than I am of anything else."

Mama doesn't understand me at all. No one understands me, and they don't get that what I'm doing is for *our family*. I'm not doing anything bad! I help the group with normal stuff, and they reward me and my friends. And if it wasn't for that money, we wouldn't be able to buy food or Mama's medicine.

Mama poured out tea from the pot that she'd put on the fire, smiling even though her face looked sad. That smile stayed with me, and, later, it was the first thing I thought about every time I remembered Mama.

Before I went to bed, I crept into the kitchen. There, I took the bag out of the cupboard and hid it really well, among the tires out in the yard. Then I went back, lay on my bed, and stared at the ceiling for a long time, until I finally fell asleep. In the morning, I went out like I always did, carrying the bag wrapped up under Omar's jacket. I'd borrowed his watch to keep track of how long I was gone, and I'd put on his jacket because it was so big on me that I could keep my stuff hidden in there without anyone noticing.

Along the way, I stopped by the oak tree and looked at everything in the secret stash, making sure it was all still there. As I covered up the hole, I thought about how I'd share part of it with Omar and Thoraya when I got back. That would give me enough time to think up convincing answers to Omar and Mama's questions.

I met Rayan at the turnoff for our village. It didn't take long before Abu al-Harith pulled up in his jeep and drove us to the center. Dozens of boys had gotten there before us. They divided us into groups, and they asked my group of five to climb into the back of a pickup. Three armed men got in with us, and we set off.

It was fall weather, and the streets were almost empty, pocked with huge, crater-like potholes because of the shelling. I knew we were going to Raqqun, since I'd been this way before. We passed a bunch of roadblocks, but the gunmen there knew the group well. When we got to Raqqun, seeing all the buildings and stuff was pretty awful, because of all the destruction, and because it smelled so bad everywhere.

I was really shocked when I saw the burned bodies lying not only under the rubble, but in the public squares and gardens, after the gunmen had their "retribution," as they called it. I couldn't help pinching my nose shut and closing my eyes at some of it, and the gunmen made fun of me. One of them forced me to open my eyes. He pointed at the bodies and said, in a gruff voice, "They've gotten their just deserts. This is the punishment for infidels."

Abu al-Harith stopped at a building that used to be a cultural center in Raqqun. There, a gunman who seemed to have been waiting for us walked up with four more boys. I don't know how they all found a place in the crowded truck bed, but we set off again.

"Where is this camp exactly?" I asked one of the gunmen. "We've gone a long ways."

He didn't answer. He just looked at the guy sitting next to him, and then they both burst out laughing!

"What are they joking around about?" I whispered to Rayan.

"They're not joking. They're mocking us."

"And what's so funny about us?"

He shrugged. "I don't know."

A few minutes later, the pickup stopped at the side of an empty road.

When they told us to get down and line up, I felt like something had just grabbed my heart and driven a nail into it.

"From now on," Abu al-Harith said, "you are God's chosen soldiers. And what you do, you will do for His cause. Forget your families. Forget your mothers, your fathers, your sisters, your brothers. You need to focus on just one thing—on ridding the world of unbelievers and their evils. We will defend our religion! Either we live with honor, or we die as martyrs, and our reward will be in heaven."

My knees went weak, and my feet couldn't hold me up anymore. They had tricked us. Had we been kidnapped? Were these the bad guys that Mama had told me about?!

I asked, hesitantly, "Aren't we going back to the village?"

Abu al-Harith walked up to me and said firmly, "No one will go back to the state of humiliation he was living in. You will stay with us and defend our religion."

"B-b-but," I stammered. "I didn't tell Mama, and she'll worry about me."

All the kids' eyes fixed on him, expectantly.

"Did I not say that you should forget your families?" he asked.

"I want to go back," I yelled at him, without thinking, and ran toward the truck.

One of the armed men ran after me and grabbed me, holding my arms tight, while another drove his fist into my belly. I cried from the pain. It looked like all the other boys wanted to cry, too, but their tears were frozen in their eyes.

After that, the gunmen shoved us into the back of the pickup. They drove us to an ancient fortress that was surrounded by water on three sides. As we crossed the only land route that led up to it, I remembered a school field trip we'd taken here about three years ago. We had been so happy then: singing on the bus, swaying to the music, dancing dabke in the aisle between the seats.

Back then, the sight of the citadel had dazzled us. It had looked like an island floating on the water. Our history teacher had told us that its walls were a priceless treasure. Now it was in ruins. The ancient stones had been ripped out of their places, turned into benches for sitting on. There were pits everywhere, like they were digging up the antiquities. And I was shocked to see that the museum was totally empty—it had none of the artifacts that I'd taken pictures of during our trip.

The citadel itself had been turned into the gunmen's living quarters. One part of it was for their leaders, one part of it was for the trainees, and a third part was for the kid fighters who were over eight. The fourth section was for kids under eight. They were called "the Cubs of the Falcons of Truth," and they either cleaned the place or served the adults or made the food. Some of them arranged the weapons in the warehouses.

Pickups were arriving with a bunch more kids, along with the regular gunmen. We lined up in the yard, where they gave us clothes. The worst part about it was that they were all black. Two long black shirts, two pairs of baggy black pants, six pairs of underwear and socks, and lace-up shoes. I *hate* shoelaces. Then they gave us our jobs. Most of the kids got assigned work in the kitchen, cleaning and serving, but they said that I had combat skills, so I had to join the military training. Thank God they chose Rayan to go with me. There were three other boys in our group: Hamza was sixteen, Ayham was around my age, and Ezzedine was three years younger than me.

Abu al-Mutasim, the gunman in charge of our group, told us to rest up in preparation for the start of training the next day. Before he left, he told us that he had chosen a new, serious name for each of us, for our new lives as soldiers. When he pointed at me, he said, "You are Abu al-Muthanna," as if I were some ancient general. But I wasn't used to the new name, so they had to call me "Sufyan Abu al-Muthanna."

They gave us a meal, but I didn't put a single bite into my mouth. Thoughts circled around in my mind, as wild as Qattoush chasing his tail, and I felt all mixed-up. Mama and Omar must be so worried about me, and who would tell them where I was? And what would they do when they found out I was here??

As for Rayan, he wasn't worried at all. He saw that this was a decent place to live, with clothes, food, clean water to drink, and everything he could want. "Here is better than the refugee camp," he said. He punched the mattress and pillow, then stroked them with the flat of his hand. "This is a real mattress, not some piece of cloth stuffed with rocks."

"Mama is going to worry about me so much," I said, like I was talking to myself. "And Omar's not going to be able to sleep at night. If I could just get a message to them, tell them where I am, maybe Omar could do something. He could save me."

"Don't worry about it," Rayan said coldly. "Nothing's going to happen to them. It's fine."

After the maghrib prayer at sunset, they asked us to stay and listen to a sermon by a sheikh who was sitting in a wheelchair. Later, Abu al-Mutasim told me that the sheikh had been a fighter out in the field, but a bullet had struck him in the spine. After that, he couldn't walk.

The sheikh said that it was a blessing from God that we now found ourselves in the ranks of the Falcons of Truth, and that implementing religious law and ruling by it was a divine command that we had to obey without question or hesitation. And, if anyone failed to do so, his punishment would be death.

I stopped listening to the sheikh, since the voice inside me was louder: They kidnapped me, lied to me, and tricked me. Was that how you implemented God's law?? After the isha evening prayer, the square was filled with gunmen. Some of them had just gotten there, and it looked like they had been out on a mission. Their loud laughter drowned out whatever they were saying. I saw a bunch of them putting white pills into water or juice, and after that they changed—their voices grew loud as they sang passionate hymns, and they fired their guns into the air.

# Chapter Eleven

I sat in a dark corner and stayed silent. Abu al-Mutasim walked up to me while he was wrapping a black bandanna around his head, and he asked me to follow him. There was a man waiting for us. He had a long scar down his face that looked like a single stroke from a knife. Abu al-Mutasim introduced me with my new name, "Abu al-Muthanna," and the man walked up and put his giant hand on my shoulder, shaking me as he said, "I'm in charge here. I'm Abu al-Bara, and I've heard about your skills as a sniper. Tomorrow morning, I want to see it for myself."

I nodded, and he motioned for me to sit down on a big boulder that was covered with a cloth. He tried to make me feel more comfortable with him, saying, "I know you're scared now. But I promise you, that's going to change as the days go by. You'll see that God loves you, and that's why He called you to be with us."

I looked him right in the eye. "God didn't call me. You kidnapped me."

"I seek forgiveness from the Almighty God. Don't you believe that God makes us servants to one another? We have enlisted you to join us, yes, so that you might find honor in this world and Paradise in the hereafter— one as vast as the heavens and the earth." Then he added, "And while you're with us, you can take your rightful revenge on the unbelievers who killed your father."

My eyes widened. "You knew my father?"

He was silent for a long moment. "No. But the warriors who brought you here told me your story."

"Did they tell you that I have a sick mother, an older brother, and a little sister who all need me to be with them?"

He busied himself rearranging his bandanna before he said, "Don't worry. With God's help, we'll take care of your family."

"What's my guarantee of that?"

He dropped his facade and gave me an angry glare. "You will follow orders. Your commitment to us is the only guarantee you have that we protect your life and the lives of your family."

I went back to my quarters. When I walked in, I was silent, lost in my thoughts. It seemed like everyone in the dorm was afraid of everyone else and trying to avoid them. I whispered what I was thinking to Rayan, and he said, "I told you, don't worry."

Rayan fell asleep first, and he was followed by Ezze-dine. Ayham was busy arranging all the stuff he'd brought with him, while Hamza spent the whole night cleaning and polishing his gun, as if it was the most precious thing in the world. I wrapped myself up in the blanket and lay there, staring at the ceiling, remembering everything that had happened. The heavy sounds of bombs and the whiz of bullets echoed loudly in my head, mixed in with people's screams and the gunmen's long sermons. I tried to remember something nice, anything that could give me a little relief, but I couldn't find a single thing except Baba's face.

Once, I had asked Baba about the secret behind his and my grandfather's and my great-grandfather's interest in hunting. He told me, "More than a hundred years ago, hunting saved people from a famine that came during the reign of Jamal Pasha. And so the skills needed to hunt were passed down, from one generation to the next, as a reminder of how valuable it could be in a crisis."

At the time, it felt like Baba was exaggerating. Famine was something that had happened in the long-ago past. I hadn't known that, after a hundred years, it would come again because of the war . . . this war that had destroyed our safe lives.

Still, even if I hadn't worried about a famine, I'd liked hunting a lot. I'd bought a plastic rifle, and I'd used it to practice shooting at things. Now, my memories of the stuff I had done with Baba kept my soul strong. "You're my great hero," he'd told me, stroking my hair with his palm. I had given him a proud smile.

Abu al-Mutasim woke us up before dawn. I got up right away and Rayan followed, while Hamza needed three violent shakes to get out of bed. And as for Ezzedine and Ayham, Abu al-Mutasim had to pour a bucket of water over their heads, before saying in a gruff voice, "Get your clothes on, get ready for prayers, eat breakfast, and then we'll meet up on the training field."

The dining hall was also divided up, like the sleeping quarters at the citadel. There was one place for the gunmen, one place for the boys, and a third for the little kids. The hall was filled with rectangular wooden tables that had plates of butter, halvah, jam, and honey on them. I sat down in silence. I didn't have any appetite, so I just drank a cup of black tea to wet my dry throat. I looked over at the little kids' section—most of them looked six or maybe seven years old. I remembered Thoraya, and I felt something sharp dig into my chest. Were these the "Cubs" that Abu al-Mutasim had told us about? They were young enough to start squabbling because the cheese in front of one of them was smaller than another kid's, or because one of them didn't like the color of his cup!

After breakfast, the men took us out into the yard outside the citadel. Abu al-Mutasim was there waiting for us. He was surrounded by everything we needed for training: weapons, big cutters to help us get through the metal fencing at roadblocks, sandbags, and poles stuck into the ground, so we could aim at a target. It reminded me of the American action movies I used to watch, dubbed into Arabic.

At seven o'clock, they divided us up by age, putting us into three sections. We all had on our black shirts and baggy black pants, which were the Falcons of Truth uniform, and we all did the same training exercises: each of us had to jump over barriers, crawl on our stomachs with a machine gun on our backs, and run through burning tires. Any kid who complained or looked tired got a kick to the stomach or a punch in the chest, and then he'd have to work even harder. It wasn't long before all of us trainees looked like we were on the verge of a breakdown, especially the younger ones.

After the first training session was over, Abu al-Bara waved me over. I was so exhausted that I couldn't even speak. My whole body was sweaty, my clothes were grimy, and, even though my stomach was empty, I felt like I could throw up, I was so tired. He tossed the machine gun at me. It was hard for me to pick it up with my wobbly arms.

"Come on," he said. "Show me what you've got."

He nodded over toward a row of black stones that were sitting on the fence, and I understood that he wanted me to hit them—not the big poles we'd been training on.

I held the machine gun steady. I had to prove I was good at this, so that Abu al-Bara would keep his word and take care of my family. Then maybe I could convince him to let me visit them.

I hit a stone with the very first shot, and then I did it again, and the rest of the stones fell one by one. The whole time, the gunmen were cheering and clapping. I heard someone say, "This boy has skills way beyond the others his age."

Abu al-Bara gave me a joyful shake. "By God, you're a treasure! From now on, you'll be teaching the other soldiers about sniping."

It wasn't like I'd thought it would be—his words didn't make me feel more secure. After all, these men had made me promises before, and they hadn't kept them. My worries about my family had only grown bigger and bigger and bigger, until they almost overwhelmed me. I had to find a way to tell Mama and Omar where I was. I had to get in touch with them, but how?

# Chapter Twelve

In the citadel, we were cut off from the world. There were no phones, no visits, and no way for us to find out what was going on with our parents, or for them to hear what was going on with us. Our instructions were strict: we had to forget about the outside world and everything in it.

The land bridge that connected the citadel to the rest of the world was guarded by armed men, and there were no boats or skiffs along the three sides filled in with water. Even if one of us thought about getting past the walls, he'd never find a rope to grab hold of.

But I didn't let myself fall into despair. I wasn't a kid anymore, and I had to find a way to reach my family. I had to take advantage of the people around me. After all, Abu al-Mutasim said that they were some of the best and strongest boys at the citadel.

So I started to make friends with the other boys in our dorm room. I knew that Hamza, the oldest of us, had come here of his own free will. He had joined up with a bunch of different armed factions before he'd ended up with the Falcons of Truth. There were scars and wounds all over his pale, round face, and even more on his strong-looking arms, which were a lot more muscular than the arms of other boys his age—a lot more muscular than my brother Omar's, for instance. Hamza must have worked out a lot. He was good at fighting too. He knew about all kinds of guns, plus how to make hand grenades.

I noticed that he didn't join us for religion lessons, and he didn't come to listen to the sermons either. Once, while he was cleaning his gun, I asked him, "Why don't you come with us?"

He was chewing on a piece of wood like it was gum, and he said, "I came here to fight and get my monthly salary."

"So, like, you didn't come to be a martyr and go to heaven, like the sheikh says?"

He spat out the piece of wood that was in his mouth. "I fight with whoever pays me the most. Here on the earth, not in heaven."

Surprised, I said, "So you're like, not a believer? Are you a heretic?"

He didn't answer, and just kept cleaning his gun. Then, when he noticed I was staring at the wounds on his face and hands, he looked up in annoyance. "Are you going to just sit around watching me? Don't you have anything to do?"

"Your eyes are the same color as my friend Salma's," I said. He didn't ask me who Salma was. He just flashed me a small, sympathetic smile and went back to cleaning his gun.

I was really surprised by how Hamza got everything he wanted, and how he didn't have to do the things we had to do. He was the only one who was allowed to wear whatever he wanted, the only one in our dorm who dared to miss religion lessons, and the only one who could call his family once a week. He was also the only one with a wallet full of money.

I knew from Ezzedine that Hamza was the oldest kid in his family, and that he had four younger sisters and a three-year-old brother. I also found out that Hamza's father had cancer. So I assumed that Hamza must have come here because he needed the money.

I didn't like Hamza. He was sarcastic and moody, and that made me unsure about coming up and asking him anything.

As for Ezzedine, he believed every single word he heard from the Falcons of Truth. Later, I found out that the sheikh in the wheelchair—the one who preached to us after the maghrib prayers—was his father, and that his mom was from a foreign country. His dad had snatched him and his sister away from her when she refused to come with him to fight.

Ezzedine was really weird. It seemed like the only things he ever thought about were whether something was allowed or whether it was a sin. But then I found out that sometimes he mixed the two up and did the things that the Falcons of Truth said were a sin. If he was discovered, he would always deny it.

Ezzedine had come to the citadel after his dad had been injured, when they'd sent his dad here to do different jobs because of his injuries, like giving sermons and religion lessons. For a kid who was only nine, Ezzedine had an amazing ability to draw maps. It was like nothing I'd ever seen—even better than the boy who had been top of my class, who could draw a map of the world from memory. Later, I found out that Ezzedine was crazy about drawing, but he did it in secret because it was considered a "sin" here. He wasn't good at tying his shoes, and every time I saw him, I remembered my brother Omar bending down to tie my shoes, asking, "When are you going to learn to tie them yourself?"

As for Ayham, he was thirteen, and he'd come from the city. The rest of his family had died in the bombings, and he was the only one who'd survived. He had managed to escape into a forest with a group of boys. There, the Falcons of Truth had caught them and brought them to the citadel. Ayham was smart, and he learned fast. He told me that, out there in the woods, he'd only barely escaped death. When the gunmen had surrounded his group, he was afraid that they were going to kill him on charges of treason, even though he didn't actually know what *treason* meant. He'd looked at the knives and machetes they were carrying and said he could make them iron tools to fight with. One of the boys with him caught on, and he said that he could cook for them, because he was good at cooking.

Ayham smiled. "Honestly, I didn't know how to make anything. Back in our family's blacksmithing workshop, I used to make coffee and tea and clean up the place."

I didn't think that the Falcons of Truth would have actually killed Ayham, or any of the kids who were with him. It was like Mama said—they needed more children: to serve them, to work as spies, and sometimes to be fighters. Once, I asked Ayham why the Falcons of Truth used swords when they had a warehouse filled with advanced weapons. He said they preferred swords because that made them look like ancient warriors.

The five of us—me, Rayan, Ayham, Hamza, and Ezzedine—were given special treatment. When I asked why, Abu al-Mutasim told me it was because we were among the "elite." He said that some of the Falcons of Truth were specially chosen because they had skills beyond those of an ordinary gunman. And these skills helped in the war against the unbelievers. When I still didn't quite get it, he explained, "The elite are the best and brightest of the recruits. You should be happy about it."

But I was *not* happy!

Out of all the boys in our dorm, Ayham was the one I liked best. Despite everything, he was cheerful. Sometimes, he'd sing in a low voice that was almost a whisper, since Abu al-Bara had banned singing, even though the gunmen sang and shot off their guns after the nighttime prayers. I smiled and told Ayham that his voice was amazing, and that if he was in a song competition like *The Voice Kids*, he'd totally win first place. He laughed and said, "I'm already on a show called *The Fighting Kids*."

But even though Ayham was cheerful, I could see he carried a huge anger that looked like it could blow up the whole world if it got the opportunity. He was always talking about death. Once, I asked him, "Why do you talk about death so much?"

He said, "If your family had died in the bombing, right in front of your eyes, and if you were the only one who survived—well, then you'd understand."

"Baba was martyred right in front of me," I said. "And my uncle too." After that, we were silent for a long time. What we'd been through was indescribable. Nobody who hadn't lived through something like it could really feel our sadness, pain, and the fury we felt toward the whole unfair world.

# Chapter Thirteen

I told Ayham that I had to find a way to let my family know I was okay. He suggested that I could ask Hamza for help. I had thought about it, but there was no way Hamza would do anything for me without getting paid.

"Don't worry," Ayham said. "I'll help you cut a deal with Hamza."

"How?"

"You'll do ten chores for him, whatever he asks for. And in exchange, he'll call your mother this week instead of calling *his* mother. So actually, it's two requests."

"Do you really think he'll say yes?"

"I don't know. We'll have to ask him. But if I were him, I'd do it."

Hamza stepped into the dorm room and threw his things on his bed. Then he sat down near us. Ayham poked me and whispered, "Go on."

"Hamza," I said, hesitantly, "I want you to do me a favor." I added, "And I'll do ten things for you, whatever you ask."

"Okay, let's give it a go," he said rudely. "Go on, take off my shoes, wash my feet and my clothes, and then make my bed."

The idea of washing his feet was gross, but I said, "Okay." But before I could get up to do what he'd asked, he took a quick look at my face and said, "Ha, yeah. And what do you want?"

"I'll give you my mama's number, and then you can call her and tell her where I am. And tell her I'm doing okay, and that I'll be home soon."

He said nothing, just gave his head a helpless shake.

"Hamza, please, I'm begging you. I'll do twenty things for you."

Hamza spat out the small piece of plastic that had been in his mouth. "Are you some kind of idiot? How am I going to call your mother without every fighter in the whole place knowing about it? They let me call, yeah. But they make me put it on speaker, so they can hear every single syllable both me and my family say."

His answer made me despair. I dragged myself back to my spot and sat facing the wall . . . It was as if my whole world had become a wall.

After a while, I felt a hand on my shoulder. It was Ayham.

"You have to run away," he said, taking a piece of paper out of his pocket. On it, there was a carefully drawn map. I realized he must have taken it from

Ezzedine, since Ezzedine made maps of everything—even of the spots where the pigeons nested in the citadel wall.

Ayham pointed down at the paper. "You see the drawing of the truck here? That's the supplies truck. This black line, that's the route it takes, and this square on the left—that's the storehouse where they keep the food. That's what Ezzedine told me when I saw him with this paper. When he went out, I dug around in his stuff and took it without him knowing."

"Do you really think I'll make it?" I asked uneasily.

"Yeah, of course you'll make it. We'll watch the warehouse until we know when the truck is coming, and we'll make sure everything on the map is correct."

"Then come with me," I said, pleading.

"I don't have a family to go back to," he said, shrugging sadly. I didn't know what I could say to change his mind.

We watched the storage space for days. We knew that the truck came once a week, but it didn't come on any specific day, so I had to be sure to have my things in place every day, so I'd be ready when the moment came.

One evening, I don't know when—I mean, I didn't know the dates anymore—Ayham rushed into the dorm, panting. He told me the truck was here. I put on my black clothes, which would help hide me in the dark night, with Omar's fleece jacket underneath, since the weather was cold. I took my bag and went out to the yard, where the gunmen were still up, as usual. Ayham kept an eye out for anything that might be dangerous. I hunkered down in a corner, near where they were unloading the truck, and at the right moment I jumped into one of the empty wooden crates in the back of the truck and curled up like a hedgehog. My heart was going about a million beats a minute, so fast it was almost flying out of my rib cage. I put a hand over my mouth and held my breath as much as I could. I stayed that way until the truck started to move. Then I heaved out a deep breath, as if I'd been in a coma.

At least an hour passed before I dared to look up and breathe normally. It was really dark, and the road was empty, and I didn't hear anything except the sound of the truck's engine and a few dogs barking. I had to get somewhere safe before I could leave my hiding spot. The truck slowed down and stopped, and I thought, This is my chance. But as soon as I got up, I heard footsteps coming toward me. I curled back up inside the box, but they spotted me.

Then I heard the driver on the phone. "We caught him . . . I can get rid of him real easy . . . The kid's a traitor . . . Okay . . . Yeah, if that's what you want."

I shivered. What did the person on the other end want?

The man who was with the driver yanked me out of the truck like he was pulling out a piece of paper.

He threw me on the ground, hard, and ordered me to sit still while he tied up my hands. The driver, whose face was covered by a black scarf, walked up. He stood right in front of me and put his gun to my head. I closed my eyes and died of fright a thousand times before I heard the sound of the bullet.

# PART THREE

## OMAR

# Chapter Fourteen

We searched everywhere for Sufyan and Rayan, but we couldn't find any trace of them. It seemed like Sufyan had planned to run away, since he'd taken his clothes and other things with him. But even though there was no sign that Sufyan had been kidnapped or harmed in any way, I still felt sure that he had been.

The sounds of explosions and shelling boomed out near our village, rattling the windows. Even so, people went on searching with us all through the night. Some waited inside the narrow alleyways of the camp, while others went out to the nearby orchards to search among the trees and in the forest. Still others searched down the main roads. I ran from one place to the next. Sometimes, I'd be out on the streets looking for Sufyan. Other times, I'd race out past the village. But each time, I'd come back disappointed.

Everyone was tired and overwhelmed. A dark cloud hung over the village, like the cloud that comes after a funeral, when you're mourning someone. We stopped hearing the sounds of bullets and explosions and the roaring of planes. I sat down near the door to our aunt's house, not knowing what to do. I heard soft footsteps coming closer, and when I looked up, I saw Salma. As she walked toward me, she said, "Omar, I don't want you to think that I helped Sufyan this time. My heart aches just like yours that he's gone. But he'll come back."

"He didn't tell you where he was going? And he didn't ask you for any money?"

"No," she said. "But once I heard him talking with his friends about a job that would earn them money. And I saw Rayan with a new phone that he tried to hide from me."

"That's what I thought," I mumbled to myself, before I started to cry. "I'm scared that one of the gangs recruited him and then took him away."

Still, after hearing what Salma knew, I felt a little hope—like I might be able to catch the start of a thread that would lead me to Sufyan. I decided to look for the Jeep that I'd seen him riding in once with his friends. If that car came back to our village, then I could follow it, and it would take me to him. Or, if it didn't come back, then I would go out and search for him everywhere.

I came home with the first streaks of dawn light. Everyone was in the big living room except for my mother. I found her sitting on a prayer rug, loudly praying and sobbing. I told her I would go to Raqqun, since Sufyan might have gone back to our house, just like last time. She asked me to wait until later in the day, when there would be more people around, because if I left early in the morning, I might run into armed gangs in the streets. People had started to worry about the violent clashes coming to our village, since the sounds of bullets and explosions were getting closer and closer.

Then, at nine in the morning, we heard strange sounds coming from the public square near the camp— screaming and weeping, mixed up with the loud engines of military vehicles—so we went out to investigate. When we got there, we saw that armed men with the gang that called itself the Falcons of Truth had come to raid the refugee camp. They were stealing people's basic supplies and anything else that might be of use to them. And, after they had finished with the refugee camp, they headed toward the houses, where they broke, destroyed, and burned everything in sight. Then they ordered us to gather in the large public square. Everyone obeyed, since the Falcons of Truth men were carrying pistols, machine guns, swords, and daggers.

My mother stood at the front of the crowd, straight and tall, glaring at them as fiercely as a lioness, while little Thoraya clung to her back. I stood beside Mama and stretched out a hand to clasp my sister's tiny palm, which was as cold as a chunk of ice. I knew that she was frozen with fear, so I gently squeezed her hand and whispered, "We're okay."

Then these Falcons of Truth started to show off in front of everybody. They stood side-by-side with their huge bodies, their thick beards, and their long hair, looking like a flock of crows that had suddenly dropped down out of the sky to land among us. One of them strode up and chose three young men from the people who lived in the camp. I recognized their faces, but had never talked with any of them. The gunmen dragged the young men into the middle of the square, tied them up, and made them kneel. Then one of the gunmen grabbed the megaphone. He said, in a strange, garbled Arabic, "We have heard it said that these misguided unbelievers have raised their words against us. Therefore, we will judge them now, as we stand here before you, and then we will impose upon them a punishment."

The scene was horrifying. The man kept shouting over the megaphone, saying things that sounded like quotes from ancient books. After he had finished his sermon, he said that their chief justice had reached a verdict about what should happen to these young men. Another gunman approached them. He had pulled a scarf up over his mouth and covered the rest of his face with a black mask, so that only his eyes were visible. He took the megaphone and said, "After deliberations, we have decided on a verdict: to sentence these traitors to death."

I don't know what trial or what deliberations he was talking about, since the three men hadn't spoken a single world. For a moment, it felt like time had stopped. Mama stayed where she was, pressing a hand to her side, while her other hand covered her mouth in terror. The young men sat meekly, not asking to be saved, but begging only for a merciful death, while the armed men loomed over them like giants.

The Falcons of Truth men looked like the thugs you saw in violent foreign movies. My heart wobbled—this was the first time I had ever witnessed such a crazy thing with my own eyes, although later, as the war went on, these sorts of scenes would happen more and more often.

The masked man pointed to three of his soldiers, who were all still kids. These kids, wearing black and with their headbands tied tight around their foreheads, walked up so that each one stood behind a tied-up young man. Each of the child soldiers aimed his revolver at the head of the young man who was in front of him. For a moment, I imagined I could see Sufyan's face among those armed children! I closed my eyes and allowed my tears to rush out, wishing the ground would open up and take me away from all of this. The masked man spoke loudly to his child soldiers, "I will start counting, and when I get to three, you'll shoot."

"One . . . two . . . th—"

But before he could finish counting, my mother had raced toward him, begging him to pardon the young men. The man refused, mocking her. She shouted, "*You* are the unbelievers, not them. *You* are the traitors." The masked man pushed her off him with his boot, then pointed his weapon at her. At that moment, I ran over to put myself in front of her. I heard Thoraya scream. My little sister fell down, sobbing, and I saw Salma pick her up and cover Thoraya's whole head so that she wouldn't see or hear anything. Thoraya was crying . . . and Salma was crying.

I threw my body around my mother's, trying to protect her from the gunmen's blows. The crowd had gone completely silent. "We will punish the traitors and apostates first," the masked man said, aiming his rifle at us. "And then we'll attend to our business with you."

Mama was coughing and spitting up blood, so I begged the masked man, "Please, let my mother go."

"Why would I?" he asked brusquely.

"Because she didn't hurt any of you."

"We didn't come here to hurt anyone either," he said. "We came to vanquish evil and to enforce God's law and God's truth."

Before he went back to his count, I shouted without thinking, "What kind of law are you talking about? You and your group are bullying us with your guns . . . God's law doesn't allow you to kill innocent people."

He walked toward me, grabbed the back of my shirt, and lifted me up so that we were eye to eye. Then he said,

"There are two things that you're going to remember, even after I kill you with my own two hands. You're going to remember my eyes, for one. And you're going to remember the sound of the bullets as they smash into your head."

In that moment, I thought only of death. But this was not my time to die.

I would have been so grateful if I could've held back my tears! The masked man went on threatening me, while I thought, This is the first time in my life that I ever stood up and challenged somebody. And it will probably be the last one too.

When the masked man finished counting to three, I heard three shots. After that, three innocent young men fell to the ground. I watched the gunmen drag the corpses and hang them up on the branches of a tree. I knew that now, it was Mama's and my turn. I prayed to God with all the fierceness in my heart, "Please God, protect us. You are the only one who can save us. Please, God, please."

Then I heard the breathless voice of Salma's father. He must have just gotten here. He hurried up to the masked man and begged him to pardon us. After brief negotiations, he took a bag out of his pocket and handed it to the masked man. After the man stuffed the bag into his pocket, he nodded, then ordered his soldiers to get out of the village square and leave us be. He spat in our direction and said, "Next time, things won't go so easy for you."

I looked over at Salma's father. There were no words that could possibly express how grateful I felt. I walked over and thanked him, and he patted my shoulder with one hand and wiped his tears with the other, repeating several times, "If I'd come sooner, I could have saved those young men."

After the gunmen left, people helped us get back home. Mama had collapsed from the pain, and I felt a tingling sensation in every single atom of my bones. "The nightmare has reached our village," Auntie Sajida said, putting a damp cloth on my arm while Thoraya curled up in Salma's lap. She squeezed out the cloth before putting it back on my bruised and bloodied arm. "But I won't be able to leave this house, no matter what happens."

"The gunmen are gone," Mama said, to reassure our aunt, or maybe to reassure herself. "They won't be back." She sighed and added, "They just want to use us as human shields to protect themselves from the bombings."

Mama got up, despite the pain, and said, "I'm going to take Omar and Thoraya, and get out of here. We'll head up to any safe place near the border."

"And Sufyan?" I asked anxiously.

"If we stay here, we'll starve to death, and we'll have no chance to look for your brother," she said firmly. This time, she wasn't crying.

But I refused. "I'm not leaving without him. If you want to go, you can, you and Thoraya."

Everyone was silent. Still, I could hear the roar of their thoughts.

# Chapter Fifteen

After that, I was at a loss. Mama refused to leave the village and go to a camp at the border without me, and I couldn't leave her and Thoraya surrounded by these monsters while I looked for Sufyan. But I couldn't stay either. My worries wouldn't leave me alone, and I lost all desire to eat or play with Thoraya. The dog Qattoush wasn't happy like he used to be, either, and he'd just sit under my feet all the time. He felt Sufyan's absence as much as I did.

I didn't like to wander around the village the way I had before. It was empty now, and you could smell the stench of bodies decomposing. A growing number of young men had gone missing, either arrested or killed, and more and more of the girls had been kidnapped and "married" to soldiers from the Falcons of Truth against their will. The Falcons had imposed all kinds of new punishments on people: There were punishments for those who didn't go to congregational prayers, and punishments for men who didn't shorten their pants to the three-quarters length they said was religiously correct. There were punishments for people who drew pictures, or listened to music, or hung paintings in their houses.

All this beauty was now forbidden, and anyone who did the forbidden things would be punished. A darkness settled over our land, spreading like a stain across the whole universe. I wondered: How can the sun still shine its light on us? How are the streets silent, not rejecting those men who are walking on them? How do the tree branches not wither in protest at being turned into gallows?

News bulletins rushed to report all the disasters that were happening to us. But in the middle of all that, they forgot to say one word that might comfort us!

That evening, I stretched out on the ground and looked up at the starry sky. If there were any aliens out there in the universe, they would be looking down on us earthlings with pity. They'd say, "Ahhh, what miserable creatures! How is it possible that they spend all their energy on killing one another?"

On my way back to our room, I saw our aunt listening to the news on a small radio, which was battery-operated so it worked despite the near-constant power outages. Meanwhile Mama was praying and asking God for relief as usual. Inside our room, Thoraya had fallen asleep. I went to her and gathered my little sister into my arms, and I fell asleep along with her.

In the morning, I decided that I was going to find a solution that would get us out of this situation. I washed my face, had bread and tea, changed my clothes, and went out. Before I'd crossed through the village square, I spotted Salma walking toward me, lifting up the veil that covered her face. The Falcons of Truth had ordered all women to cover their faces, and, if they disobeyed, they were imprisoned and flogged. "Hi, Omar," she said, smiling cheerfully. "I'm so glad you're here."

I gestured for her to sit down with me. "Isn't it dangerous for you to leave the house?"

She took in a deep breath. "Going out puts me in danger, sure, but staying at home was driving me *crazy*."

She smiled again, and I felt so good. It had been a while since I'd seen anyone smile like that.

"Oh, Omar! This morning, I remembered something important that could help us figure out where Sufyan is."

"What is it?" I asked eagerly.

"He told me, once, about a secret place near the oak tree where he hides his stuff."

"Let's go!"

"I can't go with you now," she said. "Mama wouldn't let me. She doesn't even know that I went out to meet with you. Plus, I'm scared the gunmen will see us and look for a reason to punish us."

"So then what?" I asked.

"We'll wait until nightfall. We'll meet up here, and then we'll go."

"Okay, agreed," I said. As I watched her walk away, I told myself, If I can get Sufyan back, then the next step is getting out of this hell and going somewhere safe.

I waited impatiently for the night to come, making sure that Mama was sound asleep. I put on a black coat and went out quietly, ashamed of myself for not telling Mama about my plans. I was acting like a thief, but I told myself that I had a good excuse, because Mama wouldn't let me go—she was like all the mothers here, sick with the terror of loss.

I found Salma waiting for me a few meters from our aunt's yard. She was wearing a long black robe. "You've got to stick next to me; I can barely see," she whispered, pulling the veil back over her face.

I nodded to reassure her. As we walked toward the tree, I was thinking about what the gunmen would do if they found us. Salma stopped me more than once, saying in a low voice: "It feels like someone's following us."

I looked around and said reassuringly, "Maybe it's just someone's pet, a cat or dog."

We kept on walking: carefully, fearfully. When we got to the tree, Salma lifted the veil off her face. She circled the trunk, trying to remember which way it was to Sufyan's hiding place. After a while, she decided on the direction, and then she started counting out her steps until she got to a collapsing stone wall. She jumped over to the other side of the wall, and I followed her. She looked around again and pointed to a place where there were three white stones, one on top of the other.

"This is it, the secret hiding spot," she said. "I remember Sufyan telling me how he'd used these stones to mark it."

We started to dig with dry tree branches. The dirt was soft, and it didn't take long before we found a cloth bag. We opened it up and saw a bunch of toys, candies, dates and juice, new clothes, and even some cash! The mystery of Sufyan's disappearance grew clearer—an armed gang must have tempted him with all these things. He had gone to them voluntarily. It had been his choice.

Suddenly, we heard a voice. "Hey, you two." We both froze in place.

If this was one of the gunmen, he would kill us right here. I didn't hear Salma cry out. I didn't hear her scream or call for help. But I did hear her gasp for breath. The two of us stayed frozen until the person whose voice it was walked up to us.

"What are you guys doing here?" Rakan said. "This stuff is mine."

"*You're* the one who's been following us this whole time?" Salma asked angrily.

"I didn't follow you," he said coldly. "I was just walking around. Aren't I allowed to walk around?"

Salma answered sharply. "You're allowed to go for a walk, sure, but not to spy on other people and follow them around."

"I can do whatever I want," Rakan said. He bent down and started to look through the things, snatching up whatever he wanted. Salma looked at me in surprise, and I whispered that I couldn't argue with him, because if we got too loud, people would hear us. She didn't seem convinced. The way she was looking at me reminded me of the way Sufyan used to look at me, so I decided to do something to change her mind.

"Rakan," I said in a firm but quiet voice. "These things belong to Sufyan, not you. Leave them, please."

"I'm not going to 'leave them, please,'" he said sarcastically. "You can't stop me. First, I'll take them. Then, I'll go inform on you to the gunmen."

I snatched the cloth bag out of Rakan's hand. But before a fight could break out between us, the sky was lit up by several planes firing missiles and dropping bombs, all at once, and the three of us dashed toward the forest. We ran at lightning speed, thinking only about survival, and even burly Rakan leapt like a deer. When we were a ways from the village, we sat down and caught our breath. Hours passed before the bombing was over. Once it was done, we walked back toward the village, but we couldn't get in, because armed men had surrounded it from all sides. They were shooting at everything that moved—they didn't even spare the cats and dogs trying to sneak across their line.

When we finally were able to get back to the oak tree, the first thing we thought about was checking on our families. Salma took out her phone and called her father, but his phone was turned off. Then she called her mother, but her phone was off, too, so I took the phone and called my mother, but she didn't answer.

We kept on going, heading away from the village. We walked for a long time, until sunlight began to appear over the horizon, and then we took cover in the shade of a large boulder. Salma's battery was about to die, so I suggested that I try my mother first, and check on everyone through her, since the first time we tried to call our families, her phone was the only one that rang. I dialed Mama's number, and I thanked God when I heard her voice. I apologized for going out without telling her, and I said I was fine and that Salma and Rakan were with me, and she should tell their families they were okay.

I told her I'd be back in the afternoon, when I thought the fighting might slow down. Mama interrupted, her words tumbling out, "No, no, don't come back. Go with Salma and Rakan, and get somewhere safe. I'll find a way to catch up with you. They're gathering up the boys and forcing them to join the fighters, and they're taking the girls and saying they're 'spoils of war.' You must not come back. Just keep running, and when you get somewhere safe, call me. I'll take care of myself and Thoraya, and I'll tell Salma and Rakan's families what happened."

"But Mama," I cut in.

"Listen to me, Omar," she said firmly. "You're a man now, so use your head. Do what I say, habibi. I'm begging you—coming back here will mean that all three of you are lost."

# Chapter Sixteen

As we walked, Salma kept tripping over her long black dress, and I heard her grumbling to herself in irritation until finally she grabbed the long robe and pulled up the bottom of it, tying it around her waist. She was wearing jeans underneath.

"You can get rid of those clothes," I suggested. "Anyway, they're just extra layers; you don't need them."

"Nice talk," she said, in a light tone. "But if one of the gunmen saw me without them, I'd be toast."

"I have an idea," I said, taking out the new stuff that Sufyan had been keeping in his bag. "Try on Sufyan's clothes."

"But those are boys' clothes."

"Yeah, I know," I said. "But if you disguise yourself in boys' clothes, then it'll be easier for you to move around with us. Plus, this way, you can get rid of those annoying robes you've got on now, and you won't be in trouble if one of the gunmen sees you."

"From now on, we'll call you our boy Hassan," Rakan said.

"You are so obnoxious," she snapped.

But when Salma put on Sufyan's ragged sweatshirt and hid her hair under a black cap, she really did look like one of the boys.

We walked through a lot of densely packed pine trees, and over needle-strewn, rocky ground, before we decided to get some rest. As soon as we lay down on the dirt beneath the trees, Rakan gathered up a pile of small stones and started throwing them at everything that moved: ants, lizards, birds up in the trees. After he'd used up everything in his hand, he asked, without looking at us, "Do you two have something to eat?" I took out some of the dates that were in Sufyan's bag, and soon we'd wolfed them all down.

The forest was peaceful. When we started walking again, all we heard was the twittering of the birds and the whistle of the wind through tree branches. The only thing that broke the calm was Rakan kicking at every single stone he came across with the toe of his shoe and humming an annoying tune.

We stopped again for a short rest, ate dates, and drank some of the juice. I knew we had to find shelter before nightfall, but even though we'd done a lot of walking, all we could see was pine forest stretching out around us.

Soon the sun was bidding the earth farewell, and little by little the sounds of crickets and owls grew louder. By the time it was dark, we still hadn't reached any particular destination. I was getting pretty scared, but I knew I couldn't show it.

"Let's stop here. Then we can keep going in the morning," Salma said, before adding with a grumble, "I'm exhausted, and my feet are all swollen."

Rakan and I didn't object—we'd been waiting for someone to suggest that we rest a bit.

"But where are we going to sleep?" Rakan asked, sounding confused.

"We'll find something that works," I told him, even though I wasn't at all sure we could find such a place! The faint moonlight led us to a rocky hillside and, within it, a small cave. The silence made the world seem very lonely, and all we could hear was the sound of our own footsteps. Rakan went in first. He didn't look anxious or afraid—instead, he actually looked excited. Rakan called for Salma to come in after him. Salma walked into the cave, and then she dashed back out in horror and surprise. Salma ran down the hill, and I heard her terrified shouting: "Help! Mama . . . Baba . . ."

I chased after her until she finally stopped. She was short of breath and panted as she said, "There's a snake . . . I saw it . . . It's big and . . . all coiled up."

Rakan laughed as he shouted from back near the cave: "Hassan the Boy is a coward."

"You really are unbearable," I shouted back at Rakan, who was obviously the cause of Salma's panic. When he walked up, I gave him a shove, but he didn't budge.

"I was only joking around," he said coldly, before adding, "Don't be scared; I'll kill it."

"No, we can't kill her," Salma protested.

"Okay, sure," Rakan said. "Leave it to kill us, then."

Salma heaved out an impatient breath. "No. She won't kill us, and we won't kill her."

"Just a minute ago you were screaming your head off because of it," Rakan said. "And now you don't want us to get rid of it. *Pfff. Girls.*"

"It's her home," Salma said. "We were the ones who intruded on her. We leave her in peace, and, in return, she'll leave us in peace."

I agreed with Salma—it wasn't fair for us to drive out the snake and take over her home. "We'll find another cave. This whole area must be full of them."

Sure enough, it wasn't long before we found another cave, but even the thought of going inside it gave us the creeps, so we decided to sleep under the pine trees and take turns on guard until morning. We drew lots, and the first shift was mine.

I picked up a big stick as a weapon, and I sat across from Salma and Rakan, who stretched out on the pine needles and thin grass as if they were sleeping on a plush mattress. I was glad to watch over them. Even though I knew I was going to have to take care of them—when I didn't even know how to take care of myself—still, it was a comfort to have company.

Baba used to tell me that, if I ever found myself out in the wilderness alone, for a long time, I should keep my cool and not panic. Well, sure I knew I had to stay calm, I just didn't know *how*. I took a few steps, carrying with me my fear, my dread, my helplessness, and the feeling that I was really lost . . . I grabbed a tree trunk and hugged it tightly, praying, "Oh God, please protect me." I felt a little better after that, but the fear didn't totally go away.

Before, I had always tried to avoid responsibility, which bothered my parents. If I ever failed to do something that she'd told me to do, Mama would ask, "When are you going to take charge of your life?"

Baba used to ask me to do things that, at the time, had seemed totally meaningless. More than once, I'd heard him whisper to Mama, "He's *got* to be more active. I love to see him reading or drawing, sure. But it's ridiculous that he hears the doorbell and doesn't move a muscle to go open it. And how can he hear his sister screaming without even asking what's wrong with her?"

As the night went on, I felt the sting of the autumn chill more and more, and I started to lose momentum. We had agreed to take turns on guard, but we never said how many hours each person would be on duty. And how could we figure it out, when we couldn't tell what time it was, since none of us was wearing a watch? I crawled over until I was close to Rakan. Then I put my head down into my arms and fell into a deep sleep. We didn't wake up until sunlight was edging over the horizon.

I seemed to have unconsciously stretched out in search of a comfortable position, putting my head on Rakan's shoulder, because I woke up to him trying to get his shoulder out from under the weight of my head. He said angrily, "You were supposed to guard us, but instead you decided to sleep!"

"I *was* guarding you," I said, my voice sluggish and tired. "I must have fallen asleep against my will."

"Don't you know how to say a single nice thing?" Salma snapped back at Rakan. "Omar's been guarding us all night, and now you're blaming him for a nap?"

"I'd rather be eaten by some predator than stay with you," Rakan said, standing and shaking the dust and pine needles out of his clothes.

"Go ahead," Salma said indifferently. "No one's going to stop you."

Rakan picked up a long stick and walked away. I called out to him, loudly, trying to get him to stop, but he insisted on going down the road alone.

"You should have been more patient," I told Salma.

"No, I'm right," she said irritably, "because I defended you!"

After Rakan had been gone a long time, I said, "Come on, let's catch up to him." Salma didn't object. I knew that, in her heart, she was worried about him too. I picked up the bag with our things in it and gripped the stick in my other hand, and we went on. But we couldn't find Rakan. Where had that boy gotten off to?

Both of us were hungry and thirsty. After we'd walked for a while, I noticed that Salma was starting to have trouble talking—her lips were so dry, they were almost sticking together. I checked the things in the bag. All we had left was ten dates and two cans of orange juice. I took out two dates for me and two for Salma, and we each devoured our share in seconds. Then we split a can of juice.

# Chapter Seventeen

I miss Mama and Baba," Salma said, as we walked on. "And I miss our house."

"Me too," I said. "I hope to God we'll go back soon."

"But I'm happy we're together," she said kindly, and then she gazed at me with a confidence that strengthened my resolve. "I believe in you, Omar."

Her words buoyed me up—it was the first time someone had ever said they believed in me. After that, Salma started humming, and she nudged me to sing along. "Come on," she said.

So I joined in.

After a while, she said, "Mama was a music teacher. Back home, we had this big, big house with a real piano in it. Baba bought it for us. He studied the arts, like Mama, but he ended up working in the textile business, because it's what my grandfather did. What did your father do?"

I looked at Salma before answering. Her expression looked so playful and childish I couldn't help but smile at her.

"Me too. I'm glad you're here with me."

"But you didn't answer my question," she said, blushing in confusion.

"My father was a physics teacher."

"I don't like physics," she said, wrinkling her nose.

"Baba used to say that physics was like our lives."

"Nah, I don't think it's like our lives," she said, shrugging. "I mean, physics says that for every action there is an equal and opposite reaction. Right? Except we didn't do anything, and look what the war has done to us." She went on, while I listened attentively. "I hate physics, because it explains everything by breaking it down into cause and effect. Everything magical turns into numbers and laws: the sunrise, the clouds blowing across the sky, the rainbow . . . even our feelings."

At that moment, I looked into her green eyes, and they seemed to be made of the kind of clear, cool water that was shadowed by trees.

But before she could say anything else, we heard a cry for help, and we ran toward the voice.

It was Rakan. He'd slid off a steep ledge and was hanging onto a trunk that jutted out over empty space—and looked like it was about to break. He was in tears, and he started begging us to save him as I tried to calm him down. I lay down at the edge and stretched out a hand, but my arm wasn't long enough to reach him. We needed a rope, but where could we find one?

"We have to do something," Salma said, undoing her belt. But it was too short.

"We need something longer and stronger," I said.

I thought maybe we could use one of the bare tree roots, and I looked all around until I found one that just might work. Then I pulled at it and pulled at it with all my strength until it tore loose from the ground. I had no idea how my frail, hungry, and thirsty body could still have that much strength in it. I ran over and extended the tip of the tree root out to Rakan, who grabbed it tightly, still bracing himself against the rocky cliff. Then Salma and I pulled with all our strength until we managed to drag him up. He fell on the ground, panting, hardly believing that he was still alive. There were cuts all over his chest and face. Gently, we helped him sit up. Then I tore off his shirt sleeve and tied it around his shoulder, trying to stop the worst of the bleeding, while Salma offered him our last can of juice to wet his tongue.

"I saw this nest at the edge, and it had some bird's eggs in it. Little spotted eggs," Rakan said, wincing in pain. "I wanted to get it, so I walked up real quiet, and then I reached out a hand toward the nest. I mean, it wasn't far, but then suddenly I slipped."

"Thank God you're safe, Rakan," I said, trying to comfort him. Salma's mind had already turned to how to get those eggs. We went back to the spot where Rakan had been. Then I gripped her hand tightly while she reached out her other one, stretching until she touched the eggs and managed to grab them. "I'm sorry, bird," she said, wiping her dirty hand off on her jeans. "I know you need your eggs, and you'll be mad when you find out they're gone. But we need them more than you do."

Rakan started to come back to his senses, finally paying attention to what was going on around him. "Eggs!" I told him, showing him the treasure in my hands.

"I like them boiled," Salma said, and a sweet smile appeared on her lips. For the first time, I saw Rakan was smiling too. We drank the eggs' liquid, and all we wanted was to eat more and more of this wet, sticky stuff. It seemed like a person lost all sense of taste when they were starving, just like they lost it if they ate way too much.

"I can't believe I just did that," Salma said cheerfully. "Me—the girl who complained when Mama served me a plate of fried eggs with pepper in it! It's like that was someone else."

She wiped her mouth with the palm of her hand. "Can you believe that I used to leave half the food on my plate, and when Mama begged me to finish it, I'd absolutely refuse, because I was scared of gaining weight? I wish I'd listened to her and stored up some fat, so that now I could burn it, one calorie at a time!"

"You can make up for it," I said. "Maybe we can catch the bird that laid those eggs, roast it, and eat it!" She laughed, and we laughed with her.

"I wish Sufyan was with us," Salma said. She added with a sigh, "He was such a good hunter. He could catch anything."

So that bad memories wouldn't overwhelm me and drag me down, I decided to share something happy. "Once," I told them, "our neighbor didn't invite Sufyan to her son's birthday party. Sufyan had argued with her son and made him really mad. So anyway, Sufyan decided to sabotage the party. He took out his pellet gun, snuck up, and he shot out all the different colored balloons that the neighbor had put up on their balcony, to decorate for the party."

"Wow, he must've gotten in really big trouble," Salma said.

"Nope," I said cheerily. "It was just the opposite—the neighbor decided to invite Sufyan to the party so he wouldn't sabotage anything else!" We laughed again.

Rakan remained silent, pressing his hand tightly to the deep gash on his shoulder. He must have hit a sharp rock, or maybe he'd slammed it into some snapped-off tree trunk. After a while, we noticed that it was hard for him to talk or cough. We helped him stand up, and he leaned on us as we kept walking toward the valley. When we'd almost reached the valley, Salma stopped and said, panting, "I think if we keep on walking, we'll find water. *Valleys often lead you to water*, or anyway, that's what the geography teacher used to say."

Salma was right, and a few hours later we found ourselves in front of a spring. The trickling sound was a magical delight. Salma ran over to drink while joking, "Maybe we'll find fish!"

Rakan stayed where he was, propped up against me. I brought him to a place close to the water, where I helped him sit down on a rock. Then I scooped up water for him in my hands, tipping it into his mouth until he had drunk his fill. After that, I cleaned out his wound as best I could. When I was done, I laid Rakan on the ground and let him sleep for a little while.

It was a warm day for autumn. Salma washed her hair and combed it with her fingers. I stood there, in the cold water, until I felt refreshed. Then we started to collect reeds, arranging them into piles where we could sleep. The whole time, we kept drinking water, trying to fight off our hunger. Then, just before sunset, Rakan's temperature started to go up. It was like his whole body was on fire, and we tried to cool it down with water, but it didn't work. Salma sat on the ground, hugging her knees against her chest in a gesture of helplessness.

# Chapter Eighteen

In the distance, I heard bells faintly ringing. I reached over and shook Salma. Then I looked into her eyes, trying to give her hope, "There are people nearby. Listen." Little by little, the bells grew louder, and they were followed by a bleating sound. Salma's eyes widened in surprise. "It's sheep. We can ask their shepherd to help us."

We left Rakan lying there and followed the source of the sound until we saw a flock of sheep lining up to drink water. We walked toward them. But before he saw us, the shepherd began to play a tune on his mizmar.

"Hello, Uncle," I called out in a friendly voice.

But he didn't look over at us. He got up and plunged his hand into the water, cupping some in his hand and drinking deeply before he washed his face and wiped it off with the end of his sleeve. We stood there and waited for his response.

"Hello there," he said, as he walked toward us. "What do you want? And where are your people?"

"We don't know where they are right now," I said. "We ran away from the bombing."

"Everyone's running away," he said in a low voice. Then he added, "Come on, come with me."

"There's a third boy with us," I said. "He's injured, and he can't move."

We all walked back to where we'd left Rakan, and then the shepherd helped us put Rakan on his donkey's back. The animal carried him until we reached the cave where the shepherd lived with his wife. It was a large cave. In front of it, they'd walled off a few small areas with stones and covered them with cloth—later, we found out they were pens for the sheep to sleep in and for raising chickens. The shepherd's wife welcomed us, and she was happy when she found out there was a girl traveling with us. "We can be friends," she said warmly, as if she wanted to make Salma feel at ease.

"But why are you staying out here?" Salma asked.

"Because of the war," said the shepherd's wife. "Our house was bombed, and our three children were buried under the rubble." As she went on, she started to cry. "Saeed, Maysoon, and Doha. We'd left them asleep in their beds and had gone to visit a neighbor. Then a heavy bombing caught us by surprise. When things calmed down, we hurried back to our house, but it was already too late. And so it was that we survived, but I wished we hadn't."

Salma came up and gave the woman a hug.

"Maysoon was your age," Umm Saeed said as she hugged Salma tightly. "God protect you."

Her tears broke my heart. In the weeks to come, the woman was very kind, and she took care of Rakan, who got a little better every day.

Once, she whispered to me, "Someone was hurting this boy. He's got old wounds from many beatings. Poor child." She added, "Was he one of the young fighters? We saw many of them on our way here."

"No," I said. "But he was always in a lot of trouble, and he liked to get in fights."

It was so good to drink sheep's milk and to eat meat and hot soup. We decided to stay until Rakan had fully recovered. Salma was happy that she could wear one of Maysoon's dresses and fix up her hair. She helped Umm Saeed milk the sheep, tidy the house, and cook the food. For my part, I helped Abu Saeed, the shepherd; I'd go out to the pastures with him in the morning, and we'd come back before sunset. I loved playing musical instruments, and he taught me to play the mizmar, although of course I couldn't do it as well as he could.

We stayed with Umm and Abu Saeed for several weeks. I don't know how many weeks exactly, since for me time was only about the sunrise and sunset, the warmth or chill of the weather.

And what was going on with my family??

I had dreams about Mama and Thoraya. Mama was collecting flowers in a huge field and arranging them in beautiful bouquets. Then I saw Thoraya running toward me, carrying a bunch of flowers, barefoot and in ragged clothes. As she got closer, I was shocked to realize that what she held in her hands was not brightly colored flowers, as I'd first thought, but brightly colored bombs. Thoraya wanted to throw them, so I grabbed hold of her and shouted at the top of my lungs, "Thorayaaaaaa, watch out!"

I woke up in terror. After that, I went out and sat in front of the animal pens until morning. The next day, we decided to leave. The start of the winter cold was hanging in the air. Um Saeed gave us water, milk, eggs, and a few loaves of bread, and Salma asked for an iron skillet and matches, saying that we would need them.

Salma put Sufyan's clothes back on, but she kept Maysoon's dress, saying it would bring her good luck. We said goodbye to the shepherd and his wife, even though they urged us to stay. It just wasn't possible—we had our own families to get back to.

Abu Saeed insisted on walking with us until we reached a high hill, and from there he told us to go south, since there was a village just a few days' walk.

This time, our journey was more comfortable. We had warm clothes to protect us from the cold, blankets to sleep on, food, and water. Most important, Salma and Rakan didn't go back to bickering with each other. Rakan's temper seemed to have lost its sharp edges, and he could even say *thank you* now.

We went on pushing through the fatigue of walking and worrying, and we kept on hoping that we'd find somewhere safe. We spent several days skirting one forest, and then crossing through others, but we didn't find the village that Abu Saeed had told us about. We must have gotten lost, since we hadn't come across any people, despite how much we'd walked.

The days passed, and we ran out of food. Then the water was gone, too. We couldn't sleep well, or for long, because the weather was so cold, and our blankets weren't thick enough to keep us warm. Rakan and Salma were on the verge of exhaustion, and I felt like I was about to collapse and give up completely—but I pulled myself together and forced myself to keep going.

I got the idea of gathering some pine nuts for us to eat. When I told Rakan, he said, "We can picture them in a salad." That brightened up Salma's face, despite her pallor.

Before we started eating, we heard a sound in the bushes. "Maybe it's some animal we can eat," Salma said. "I'll gather up some wood and light a fire."

"Maybe it's a hungry animal that wants to eat *us*," Rakan said in protest.

"Fine," she said indifferently, and gestured toward the two of us. "So how about you go and hunt that animal?"

Rakan and I crept slowly toward the source of the sound. Rakan was carrying a big rock, while I had a stout stick. I stirred up the leaves with the stick, and then Rakan pounced toward the waiting food. But then we froze in place, looking just like two statues.

# PART FOUR

## SUFYAN

# Chapter Nineteen

When I woke up, my head was pounding. I glanced down at my hands, and then I looked up all around me. I realized that the driver hadn't shot me in the head, and I hadn't died! If I were dead, then I wouldn't be able to see or move my body! I was alone in some dimly lit, bare room, probably back at the citadel. My feet were tied up with iron chains, and the chains were looped around the seat I was sitting on. I tried to yank free, but I couldn't.

Gunmen came in and beat me up: there wasn't a single place on my body that they didn't kick. Then they gave me ten lashes on my back with a belt as punishment for trying to escape. When they saw I couldn't move, two of them picked me up and threw me back into my dorm room. None of the other boys came anywhere near me. Maybe they had been ordered to stay away from me, and so they were scared of being punished. I curled up in pain.

At dawn, Ayham walked up cautiously and covered me with a sheet, and then he put a hand gently on the top of my head. He whispered, "Abu al-Bara was asking for you. I guess he wanted you for something, and that's how they discovered your escape. They searched our room and found Ezzedine's maps. They tore a bunch of them up and beat him. Poor kid, it wasn't his fault. Can you believe that his father, the sheikh who never stops saying, 'This is halal, this is haram,' beat him up with no mercy when they found a drawing of a woman's face in Ezzedine's stuff? We found out later it was his foreign mother." Ayham went on, "I thought about admitting what we'd done, but I was too scared." Then he burst into tears. "I'm so glad they didn't kill you."

"Not yet." I said it sarcastically, even though I was so exhausted I could barely speak.

I drank some water and felt the chill as it dropped into my empty stomach. Then I ate a few dates that Ayham had saved for me and got back a little of my energy. Ayham helped me wash my face, and he dried it off with the edge of his shirt.

After a brief silence, he told me that there was another way I might be able to get in touch with my family without putting myself in danger. When he was doing his work for the blacksmith, he'd found out that there were a bunch of computers in one of the rooms. He suggested we try to send an email to my family, since it wasn't possible to call.

I told him I didn't know if anyone in my family even had an email address. He thought for a minute and said,

"Then send a message to any email you can find on Google—a magazine, a newspaper, or anybody, and give them your mother's phone number." I couldn't deny that I liked the idea, but I was afraid it would be discovered, since the Falcons of Truth had people who were experts with technical stuff. I had seen them acting in front of the camera, filming scenes to document what they were doing, like they were making a movie.

"No, Ayham," I said, shaking my head in despair. "I can't risk it again. At least not now."

He nodded to show he understood. "Are you in a lot of pain?"

I didn't answer. I gathered up all my strength and propped myself up against the wall. Then I said, "Once, in a school play, I had the part of the old commander Khalid ibn al-Walid. Do you know what he said right before he died?"

Ayham shook his head.

I cleared my throat as I imagined Khalid speaking from his deathbed. "There is no inch on my body that has not been run through with a sword, shot with an arrow, or stabbed with a spear. And here I am, dying on my mattress like a camel." I grew excited and said, louder, "So may the eyes of the cowards never know sleep."

I followed it with a long *ukkh* of pain, since I'd waved around my bruised and swollen arm. Ayham laughed and tried to repeat the phrase, "So may the eyes of the cowards never know sleep." I'm sure all the boys in the room must have woken up at that, but they pretended to still be asleep.

I don't know how we could laugh when our lives were so miserable!

Can sadness make you laugh?

I couldn't get out of bed, so I didn't go to breakfast. Abu al-Mutasim came and dragged me, still struggling, over to a room where Abu al-Bara was waiting for us. My bones had been crushed, and it felt like my head was about to explode. Abu al-Bara gave me a white pill, like the ones the gunmen put in their drinks when they stayed up at night. He said it would take care of the pain. I needed medicine that would dull the pain, but I still didn't take it, because it was too hard for me to swallow pills. Back at home, I always took liquid medicine.

"This time, we are satisfied simply to punish you, since you are one of the elite," Abu al-Bara said. "But if something like this happens again, neither you nor your family will be spared."

"But you promised you wouldn't hurt them," I said hoarsely.

"And you promised to stay with us," he said in a mocking tone.

"I have to tell my family where I am."

"Soon, soon," he said. "Just don't do that again. Then you'll see, everything will be fine."

"Do you know my family? You always talk about Baba as if you knew him. Did you?"

"I didn't . . . know him," he said hesitantly. Then he added, "But whoever has a child as stubborn as you must be stubborn too."

It took days for me to recover. Little by little, the wounds on my body started to heal. Because of my attempted escape, they stepped up my religious awareness program, and the sheikh gave me private lessons, where he talked about the heroism of the Falcons of Truth, and how they were protecting the nation, and how we all had to fight the unbelievers.

In the beginning, these words didn't affect me much. I mean, sure, I'd like to live in the kind of city the sheikh was describing in his over-the-top way, one that was filled with only goodness. But I'm old enough to know that there's no such city in real life. And even if a city like that *did* exist, life there would be weird, and it would probably be boring. But as time passed, I started to repeat what the sheikh was saying, and to do what he suggested. His words took over my mind so much that, during my training sessions, I recited the chants I had learned by heart.

One day, I was sitting down in the dining hall at one of the far tables, because I wanted to be alone. Rayan came in carrying a white cat and waved at me. I didn't wave back or anything, because I didn't want to encourage him to join me. Then Ayham came in. As soon as he saw me, he started walking toward my table. I gestured for him to go away, but he didn't seem to notice. I wasn't in a mood to talk, but Ayham was the type who didn't care about anybody else's bad mood. He sat down next to me and said, "Next time, I'll make you something special for your escape."

"What's that?" I said sarcastically. "Are you going to make me an airplane out of iron?"

He laughed. "No, a bulletproof vest, like the armor of Khalid ibn al-Walid."

Against my will, I smiled. Ayham really could make me feel better.

"Listen," he said. "You need to have a better plan."

I was listening, and he said, "There's only one entrance to the citadel by land, and it's guarded by heavy security. The water's dangerous, and you'll never get across it. Plus, even if you did, they'd go after you like they did last time. And if they couldn't catch you, then they'd go after your family. But you know all that." I nodded, and he continued, "Your only way out of here is through Abu al-Bara. They're using us as best they can, and we can do the same—use them too."

"We? Does that mean you're thinking about running away with me?"

"No, no," he said. "I'm not running away. I want to get revenge on the people who killed my family."

"You know who did it?"

"Yeah. The ones with the planes that bombed my house."

"Okay, sure, I see," I said. "So you're using them to get revenge on the people who killed your family."

He nodded. "Exactly. And you can use them in some other way. You just have to earn their trust, and then they'll let you move around like you want."

When Ezzedine walked up, we stopped talking. Everyone said he was a snitch, although, after what happened during my escape, I'd started to doubt that.

"Tomorrow we're going out to the battlefield," Ezzedine said eagerly. "My father told me that Abu al-Bara is going to take the elite to the battlefield, and that this will be our chance to get closer to God." Ezzedine talked exactly like his father. Even though he was still little, he'd memorized a whole bunch of the expressions and sayings of the Falcons of Truth. Sometimes, he even acted like them.

"It seems that your sources of information are endless," Ayham said sarcastically, which made Ezzedine mad, so he turned around and left. Only a couple hours later, we got the official word about what Ezzedine had already told us. Abu al-Mutasim stressed that we should get ourselves ready and prepare our weapons.

I watched Ezzedine, who was busy arranging his stuff. He squirreled away his stacks of papers in a spot at the bottom of the wardrobe, and then he covered them up with a plank of wood. He must have done that so he wouldn't be punished like last time.

I walked up, and he hurriedly shut the wardrobe door and gave me a fierce stare. "I'm not a snitch," I said, to put his mind at ease. "I just want to see your drawings."

I could see that he was going to say no, so I promised him gently, "I swear that I won't tell anyone. I have a little sister who loves to draw."

He looked at my face for a second before saying, "Okay, I'll believe you . . . this time."

Then he pulled out his papers and said they were maps he'd made of every place he ever went.

"Do you draw anything other than maps?"

He moved his head around in some gesture that wasn't a *yes* or a *no*.

"Are you thinking of going away?" I asked. "Somewhere far from here?"

But he stayed silent.

Still, I felt encouraged, and said, "I'm thinking about it too."

As Ezzedine took the papers back from me and returned them carefully to where they'd been, one fell out—a black-and-white drawing of a woman's face. It looked like it had been ripped up, but then he'd somehow taped the many small pieces back together again. Although there were still a few spots that were missing.

"She's a beautiful woman," I said. "Is that your mother? Do you draw maps to get back to her?"

He shouted at me with a monstrous anger, "That's none of your business! Get away from me." He threw himself against me and started hitting me as hard as he could, shouting, "Get away from me, get away from me." Hamza came over and pulled him off me, holding him back until he'd calmed down.

Privately, Hamza told me that Ezzedine had been having these nervous tantrums ever since his sister had gone off on a suicide mission. A few minutes later, Ezzedine was lying on his bed, repeating like a hypnotist, "I ask God for forgiveness . . . I ask God for forgiveness . . . I ask God for forgiveness."

I walked up and studied him for a long time. I felt like I needed to get angry and scream too. I wanted Omar to come and hold me tightly—to force me to stay home, the way he used to.

That night, Ezzedine picked up his mattress and came and lay down next to me. He said, in a voice that reminded me of Thoraya's, "It was Mama. She lives in France." After a few moments of silence, he added, "I haven't seen her in years and years, so I drew her the way I imagine her. Maybe she thinks I died, like my sister

Sally did. Sally was so scared before she went off to die. But Baba told her that she'd be in heaven, and that we'd join her after we die, and then we'll all be together. Do you think Mama is looking for me now?"

"Definitely," I said, putting my hand on his shoulder. "She must be looking for you every day. Mothers never give up. I have a mother, so I know."

"Do you love her?" I asked.

He nodded.

"Do you want to go back to her?"

He didn't say anything. And even though he pretended to be asleep, I could hear his quiet tears.

I flopped back down onto my mattress and stared at the ancient brown stones in the dormitory ceiling. I was the same—I drew Mama's face every night in my dreams. After Baba was martyred, she had been as solid as a rock. I missed her so much. I missed how she laughed when I did some funny pose in front of her. I missed the sound of her voice, even when she was mad, even when she said, "Boy, you're going to drive me crazy. Have mercy on your poor mother." I'm sure that Mama is looking for me and that she'll never give up. Omar too. That's what I hold onto, and that's what gives me strength.

# Chapter Twenty

In the morning, we went with a group of gunmen to Rahmoun, which is the next city after Raqqun. It took more than two hours before we stopped in one of the olive groves. There, the gunmen made camp, setting up the tents so that they'd stand up against the strong winds. Then they assigned each of us to a tent.

In the late afternoon, after asr prayers, a bunch of gunmen showed up. They were dragging a blond man with light-colored eyes. They said he was a spy, and that he was their enemy and an enemy of God. Someone set up a big camera and started filming the whole thing. They ordered us to look at the man as they carried out the sentence, but I lowered my head, keeping my eyes on the ground so I couldn't see anything. Then they dragged off the man's body and threw it into a big pit that was far from the camp.

The next morning, they took Ayham, Hamza, and Rayan to fight, and they came back in the afternoon waving their rifles and shouting victory chants. They had four prisoners with them, who they called "apostate enemies." They pulled them out of the back of a pickup, put them in a row, and tied their hands behind their backs. Then they made them kneel. Abu al-Bara called me over, handed me his gun, and said proudly, "Go on, choose your gift from among these men."

"My gift?" I asked, my voice shaking.

"Yes," he said. "This is your chance to rid the world of evil. Choose one of them and carry out the sentence."

"What did they do?" I asked.

"They're unbelievers who don't know God. They don't want us to be able to establish a state. They're the ones who killed your father and turned your family into refugees." Then he shouted, "Death to the unbelievers! Death to the unbelievers!" The gunmen chanted behind him.

Abu al-Bara placed the gun into my hand and gestured for me to carry out his order. As I held the revolver in my trembling hand, thoughts raced through my head: Why should I kill someone who's never done anything to me? This is an injustice. God has forbidden injustice. Then I closed my eyes and decided, No matter what happens, I won't kill anyone. I let the gun drop out of my hand, and I ran off, but then I tripped over a rock and fell, tumbling into the dirt. The gunmen laughed at me.

"It's all right," Abu al-Bara said. "This time, it's enough that you watch."

At the same time, four gunmen were lining up behind the prisoners, each holding their weapons. I didn't look at the faces of these "enemies" so that their eyes wouldn't chase me today and tomorrow and every minute of my life. I saw Ezzedine closing his eyes and covering his ears, so I did it, too, and I must have been crying, because at that moment I felt something hot raining down my face.

Hamza, Rayan, and Ayham stripped off their stained clothes, and then they started talking about what had happened that day as if they'd been playing FIFA. They said they were happy to get rid of the people who had killed their families and turned them into refugees. Hamza busily cleaned his gun, as if that was the most important thing in his whole life, while Rayan ate with a big appetite. He took the leftovers to feed his cats, and he put them out in the yard of the citadel when we got back. To kill people and feed cats! It was so strange!

The bombing went on all night. We heard the explosions, and then the sky shimmered and the ground shook. The sounds got louder and louder, and then they were quieter again. I wrapped my blanket around me and squeezed my eyes shut. I forced my mind to think of anything nice, and then I heard my mother singing with Thoraya in her lap . . .

I saw Baba lifting me up in his arms and putting me on his shoulders as we climbed up Mount Bishri. He laughed when I told him that the view from the tower of his shoulders was amazing. "You're better than the Eiffel Tower." When the sun started to rise, Abu al-Mutasim came, like a cold shadow, to wake us up. I hadn't slept all night, and I felt disoriented.

"Come on, training is starting," he said, kicking at the sleepers with his hard, black boots.

"I can't," I told him. "I'm too tired."

"A coward," he said, turning to glare at me. "The coward's punishment is the same as the unbeliever's. Did you know that?"

I put my hands over my ears so I wouldn't hear anything else and shouted, "I want to leave here or die!"

He grabbed me by the shoulder and dragged me out of the tent. "I can easily arrange the second one for you."

Abu al-Bara walked up and threw my clothes at me, so that they covered my face. Then he said, "You're with me. Come on, put your clothes on. We're off."

I got dressed in silence and climbed into a jeep. Abu al-Bara was sitting next to the driver. He moved his tasbih beads through his fingers as he said, "May God guide you to the path of righteousness, my son."

"I'm not your son," I whispered, feeling sick to my stomach. I hated this monster *so much*! The car took off, moving fast, and when I looked into the side mirror, I saw a bunch of other Falcons of Truth cars following behind us. We must be going to a battle, I realized. I fixed my gaze on the passenger window and, as I looked back, I saw the long roads as scars on the earth. War left you nothing but wounds. War churned sadness into the air until it was all you could breathe.

We passed Raqqun, but if it hadn't been for a traffic sign with the name written on it, I wouldn't have even known it was my city. The buildings were in shambles, the streets were destroyed, and the neighborhoods were deserted. The car turned toward al-Numan, the village where my family had fled to. My heart started to pound. Were they going to send me back to Auntie Sajida's house, or would they punish me in front of my relatives because I'd refused to join in the morning drills? Would the battle be in our village? Would I see Mama, Omar, and Thoraya again? Would they even recognize me? I was taller and thinner, and I hadn't gotten a haircut since I'd left them.

A few minutes later, we were at the village. The whole place smelled awful. Nothing had escaped the fires of war. Even the oak tree was gone—there was nothing left but its burned stump.

I begged them to let me see my family. "Now you're begging me," Abu al-Bara said cruelly. "So why did you shirk your responsibilities before? Look what the unbelievers did to the village. These are the people we asked you to fight. But in your opinion, they don't deserve punishment?"

"I'll do whatever you want," I pleaded. "I swear."

"All right," he said. "Even though you don't keep *your* promises. I'm trying to make you into a man, but here you insist on staying a child."

"I'll do whatever you want," I begged even harder. "Just let me visit my family."

Abu al-Bara moved a tooth-cleaning stick around in his mouth, and then he spat out little pieces of wood through the car window. The car made its way up toward our aunt's house. When we got there, I was stunned to see it had been destroyed. The tires were scattered everywhere, and smoke was rising from the ruins.

I jumped out of the car and ran to what was left of the house in shock. I picked up as much of the rubble as I could and threw it to the side. Unthinkingly, I shoved aside off all the tires that got in my way, until under one I found a burned-up corpse. It was my dog, Qattoush. I knelt down next to him, closed my eyes, and shouted, "Mama, Omar, Thoraya!"

Abu al-Bara grabbed my hand to pull me up, and I screamed at him like a madman, "Get away from me! I want to stay here."

I was full of rage, but I didn't cry. I couldn't believe that my family was gone, and that I'd never see them again. I had tried to come back for them. I was going to say I was sorry for all the mistakes I'd made and promise that I'd never, ever do anything to upset them again.

I clawed at the ground with my fingernails, looking for anything. I found one of Thoraya's dolls under a pile of rocks. I yanked it out, panting. Then I dusted it off and put it in my bag.

I was angry at Mama because she had decided to move us to her aunt's house in the first place. I was angry at Omar because he hadn't been strong enough to stop me from leaving.

I was angry because I'd lost my family.

I was angry at the people who had killed them for nothing, no reason at all.

Abu al-Bara came up to me and said, "You have to avenge them. You have to take your revenge. That is how you become a man."

Inside me, something broke.

# Chapter Twenty One

We went back to the camp in the olive grove. I didn't talk to anyone. I was too busy getting my weapon ready and doing target practice. That evening, I dissolved a white pill in water, celebrated with the gunmen, and sang all the anthems of theirs that I'd memorized.

As the days passed, I got used to life in the camp, where we did more and more brutal training exercises. I kept on going to the evening meetings, where the sheikh talked to us about dying in the defense of truth and religion. I started to fantasize about seeing my family again in heaven, and I dreamed of all the beautiful things that would be waiting for me there, after I'd rid the earth of the unbelievers and their evils.

Abu al-Bara convinced me he was right: "The unbelievers are not human beings. They're criminals who must be killed. We will be brutal with them until they recognize who we are. We will be their constant nightmare."

I made sure to join in all the battles, follow instructions, and shoot straight so that my bullet wouldn't miss its mark, until Abu al-Bara took me up next to him and praised me in front of everyone.

And when I got back to the camp, I'd wash my hands and eat. Then I'd sit alone and not talk to anyone.

The gunmen had more faith in me, so they assigned me to train fighters and gave me a lot of privileges. I could walk around the camp by myself. I had extra food. I stopped dreaming with my eyes open, and I got used to the smell of blood, so that it didn't make me feel like I was choking. Old memories started to fall out of my head until it was empty. I felt like my whole head had been taken off and a new head had been put in its place, filled with white pills, fiery anthems, cruelty, and the desire for revenge.

As the weather got colder, we went back to the citadel. There, I discovered that I had lost my bag—the one where I'd hidden Thoraya's doll, some of my clothes, and the watch I'd taken from Omar. I looked for it everywhere before finally I gave in to the idea that I had lost my family and every single memory of them. One night, as we were preparing for a "major" military operation— or at least, that's how Abu al-Bara described it—we discovered that the citadel had been surrounded. Abu al-Bara gathered us up and said that the unbelievers wanted to get rid of us, and that they had planes, missiles, and all the modern weapons. They wanted to destroy the citadel that stood above our heads, he said, and he ordered us to follow his instructions down to the letter.

His plan was for the men to escape through a system of ancient tunnels that lay under the citadel, while the Cubs and boys would stay aboveground. He promised us that the attacks would stop as soon as the enemies saw they were fighting a group of kids.

Just before dawn, when showers of bombs started to fall on us, and bullets were being fired right at us, we finally realized that the gunmen were using us as cover so they could escape. I told the boys with me that we had to escape, too, because if we stayed here, we'd be finished. Everyone agreed, and we started a plan to withdraw toward the tunnel.

"We shouldn't have believed them," Hamza said. "They tricked us into being human shields for them."

"What does that mean?" Ezzedine asked.

"It means that if we stay here, we'll die," Hamza said.

"But . . ." Ezzedine said, hesitantly. "Don't you want us to sacrifice ourselves, so we can get the reward?"

"What's your deal?" Hamza asked sharply, looking over at him. "Are you going to waste time chattering?"

"Okay, I'll stop talking," Ezzedine said. Then he added, "They left Baba here."

"So we'll pick him up and take him with us." Hamza sounded impatient.

"If they find out, they're going to punish us," Ezzedine said.

Rayan cut in, wheeling on Ezzedine, "Are you seriously saying that if we died like this, it would be some kind of holy sacrifice, you idiot?"

"I'm not an idiot," Ezzedine said quietly. "I have a map of the tunnel."

Rayan pulled his hand off Ezzedine, and I said, encouragingly, "Let's go get your father."

I went along with Ezzedine, and we found his father praying. We waited until he had finished, and then we asked him to come with us. But he refused, and he even tried to stop his son from coming with us, telling him that he had to sacrifice himself, just like his older sister. I was worried that Ezzedine might be swayed by his father's words, so I whispered, "If you stay here, you won't get a chance to see your mother."

Then I grabbed his hand, gave it a hard yank, and dragged him along with me as I ran toward the rest of the boys.

"I'll get some flashlights," Ayham said, and he and Hamza ran off to the warehouse where gear was stored. As for Rayan, he wanted to go collect his cats and take them with us! But I stopped him.

With the help of Ezzedine's map, we got into the tunnel. Me, Hamza, Ezzedine, Ayham, and Rayan walked in front, and the others followed behind us. We couldn't think about the dust and rocks that were falling on us from the walls, which were shaking under the heavy bombardment—we just kept going until we saw a faint light that showed we were close to the end. In the same moment, we were surprised by shots being fired from the other side.

Ezzedine quickly pointed at a side tunnel where we could escape, and we ran off in front of him as he shouted, "To the left, to the left!"

Several boys were hit, and I saw Hamza fall. He was bleeding from his side. We tried to carry or at least drag him, but the hail of bullets didn't stop, and he said firmly, "Go. Leave me." Those were his last words before he closed his eyes.

Ayham picked up Hamza's rifle and ran to the left. Ezzedine quickly pointed at a side tunnel where we could escape, but we were already way ahead of him as he shouted. Before we got there, he asked, "Was it a trap that the unbelievers set for us?"

"Yeah, it was a trap all right," Ayham said. "But it was made by guys from the Falcons of Truth."

"Why are they doing this?" Ezzedine asked, frowning as he panted. "Aren't we part of their group?"

"Maybe they know we left the citadel, and they want to punish us," I said.

"So it's like, we die and they live," Ezzedine muttered. Nobody said anything.

We kept on running, hoping that we could make it. As we ran, we heard Rayan trying to stifle groans of pain, saying, "My arm, my arm." He'd clamped his left hand over his right forearm, which he didn't seem to notice was bleeding. Ayham took off his black headband and quickly wrapped it around the wound.

"Didn't you notice that you'd been hit?" Ayham asked.

"I felt something hit my arm," Rayan said weakly. "But I thought it was just a rock."

"We should stop and take care of it," I said.

"There's no time to stop. Let's get out of here first. I can take the pain."

Our getaway seemed like an endless maze: a narrow corridor led to another, and that led to something else. We kept on going, following Ezzedine's map. Then, just when we were totally exhausted, Ezzedine said happily, "At the end of this one, we'll get to a forest!"

Little by little, daylight started to creep into the tunnel up ahead. And because it's possible to find joy even in the worst of circumstances, I cried out, "You're a hero, Ezzedine! You're our hero."

Finally, we found ourselves surrounded by a dense pine forest, with the sun peeking through the clouds. Even though we were totally worn out, we kept on walking until we were far enough that we felt safe. Then we lay down in the grass under the shade of a gnarled, old tree. That's when we noticed that, even though Rayan was keeping silent, he was in pain, and he'd lost a lot of blood. One of the boys suggested we tie another piece of cloth around the wound and pull it tight. He said that his father was a doctor, and that's what doctors did. I tore off the sleeve of Rayan's shirt, and Ayham helped me bandage up the wound.

The bleeding stopped, but then Rayan started screaming in pain, so I took out a white pill and gave it to him. I had to. I knew these pills messed up your mind, turning human beings into beasts, or something even worse than beasts. After all, a beast hunted its prey only to eat, and then it went on with its life. But as for the Falcons of Truth, they wanted us to destroy life entirely.

After we had rested for a little while, Ezzedine started flipping through his papers. He pointed at one of them and said there was a small river nearby. He added, to encourage us, "We can get there in two hours if we walk fast."

Ezzedine got up and started walking without looking back. And even though some of us doubted that he could possibly know all this stuff, and some just didn't believe what he said about the river, and some said he would hand us over to the Falcons of Truth, we all followed him. We had no other choice! And anyhow, it was true. Before noon, our ears caught the sound of water.

We ran to the river, where we drank and played as if we were at the city pool. After we'd cleaned out Rayan's arm and clothes, he asked me for another pill. I searched my pockets, but I found that the water had gotten to the pills and dissolved them. I felt relieved, even though Rayan's groaning didn't stop.

Just before sunset, we started to feel cold, so we lit a big fire and made a circle around it. Then hunger struck us, and, while we were thinking of how to get food, we saw an animal that looked like a mountain goat near the river. He was small and hopped around like a lost stray, moving from one place to another.

I snapped up Ayham's rifle and walked carefully toward the animal. When I fired my first shot, the other boys cheered, but I missed! I was furious at myself and decided to try again, and they kept cheering and clapping, even though I only hit it on the second try. Only a few seconds passed before the other boys were racing to get it and drag it back, to be our supper.

After we had eaten around the fire, we decided to sleep near the river. Ezzedine and I went looking for a good place to spend the night. On our way back, it was getting dark, and we heard strangers' voices mixed in with the voices of the other boys, so we hid behind a tree and tried to figure out what was going on before anyone noticed us.

We saw a group of men. Behind them, there were three cars that belonged to one of the international relief organizations. I knew what they were from the logo printed on sides of the cars, since I'd seen it every day on Mama's news shows. It was clear that the boys were scared, and that they didn't know what the men wanted from them. The men spoke in a bunch of different languages. In the end, they persuaded the boys to get into the cars.

"Let's go with them," Ezzedine whispered. "Then we'll get somewhere safe."

I shook my head. "No way. Maybe they're going to put them in prison. I don't want to go to prison."

"Then what are we going to do?"

Without hesitation, I said, "We run."

He looked at me. "How did they even know we were here?"

I tried to think back on everything that had happened, and to connect it to these men. "The sound of bullets must have led them to us." I closed my eyes for a long time, as guilt ate away at me. Why hadn't I thought about that? I should have been more careful.

When the three cars drove off, Ezzedine and I ran toward the cave that we'd thought would be good for sleeping in. We cleaned it up as best we could and decided to stay there until things calmed down. Then we could go out and find somewhere that was safer.

# PART FIVE

## OMAR

# Chapter Twenty Two

The two boys jumped up and attacked us, as if they were two ferocious tigers. We stumbled as we scrambled away, and then they stared at us for a few moments before they realized that we were the same as them: wandering runaways.

We told them our story, and they told us theirs: Their father had been a journalist who had published articles critical of the Falcons of Truth, and their mother had been a photographer who took the pictures that went with his articles. The Falcons of Truth gang had threatened their parents more than once. And in the end, the threats came true.

Ayman, who was thirteen, told us about all the terrible things that had happened to them. He said that their family had fled their house and driven toward their grandparents', hoping to save their lives. But on the way, they saw jeeps making a roadblock. They could see that those jeeps belonged to the Falcons of Truth.

Their father had stopped the car, telling his wife and two sons to run away toward the olive groves. Then he'd driven in the opposite direction, trying to lead the danger away from his family, but the gunmen's bullets didn't let him get far. After that, the gang chased the rest of the family down until they caught their mother and killed her. But Ayman and his brother, Tahsin, who was seven, hid among the trees and managed to escape.

They had spent days in this spot without food, and they were tired and hungry. After a short discussion with Salma and Rakan, the three of us decided to help them get to their grandparents' house.

Ayman said that their grandparents lived just behind the hill, and then he pointed south.

"Let's go," Salma said. But before she could take her first step, Ayman stopped her, saying that the path was littered with mines, all the way down to the valley.

Tahsin nodded, backing up his big brother. "Yeah, we saw a donkey walking in the valley. And then *booooooomm*. It blew up."

"Then let's go another way," I said.

"But we might have the same problem somewhere else!" Salma said.

"Okay, I have an idea," Rakan said. "I'll walk in front of you and put a rock down on every step that's safe. And if I get across, then you should walk on those rocks until we cross the valley."

I could barely believe that this was Rakan speaking. He had changed so much. Before, he used to take pleasure in hurting other kids, but now he wanted to sacrifice himself for us! I looked at him proudly and said, "No. We won't let you take the risk."

Salma stood on a large rock and said confidently, "All you boys have big muscles, right? So together you can find some heavy tree branches. Pick ones that are big and shaped like cylinders. We'll put them down, let them roll in front of us, and if they get to the bottom safely, we'll follow their lead."

"You are the best and smartest leader in the world," I said, and Salma's eyes lit up and her face went red.

We dragged one of the logs over before rolling it from the top of the hill, and we heard it explode midway down. We brought a second, a third, and a fourth trunk, repeating the process. It didn't take long to find the logs, since a lot of trees had been destroyed by the bombing. Finally, we set a huge log at the edge of the hill and let it roll, and it reached the valley floor safely. We jumped up and down, high-fiving one another while chanting happily, "We did it, we did it, we did it."

The ground was still soft from the rain, and we crossed the valley in peace. After that, we climbed up to the opposite hill. As we were walking, we heard a huge explosion behind us. We looked back, only to see what looked like the remains of some poor animal that fate had led to its end. Nothing could survive the war: not humans, not trees, not animals, not birds, and not houses.

"Why do they put these things in our path?" Tahsin asked.

"Because of the war," I said.

"But why does there have to be a war?" he asked.

"Because there are some people who want to take the land and everything on it for themselves," Salma said.

"Why don't they share it?" Tahsin asked.

"Because sharing is just and fair," I said. "And they hate justice."

He didn't seem to understand what I meant any better than he'd understood Salma. But my answer was enough to keep him quiet and stop him from asking more questions.

At the top of the hill, we said goodbye to Ayman and Tahsin, after they checked to make sure they were close to their grandparents' house. We didn't even consider going with them, since Ayman had told us that the house had no electricity.

We were trying to get to a place where there were people, so we could use their electricity to charge the phone. Then maybe someone would help us get back to our families.

Salma said quietly, as if talking to herself, "Do you think our parents are okay?"

"Yes," I said. "I'm sure they are."

"How can you be so sure when we haven't seen any of them for so long?" Rakan asked.

Salma whirled on him. "You sound like you don't even want to go back to your family!"

Rakan kicked at the ground with the toe of his shoe, and small stones flew up around us.

Salma stopped and looked into his face. "Don't you miss your mother and father?"

"He's *not* my father. He's my mother's husband." Rakan didn't meet her gaze, but kept his eyes firmly fixed on the ground.

Salma and I were both taken by surprise, since neither of us had known that before.

"Where's your father?" Salma asked.

"He lives in another country, far away, and he never asks about me. I sent him some messages, asking him to come and take me with him, but he never answered."

"Okay," I said, trying to lighten the mood. "But your stepfather who's been raising you—he's like a father."

"No," Rakan snapped. "I hate him. He yells at me, he swears at me, and he beats me, sometimes for no reason. He's a monster, not a human being."

"And your mother, won't she stand up for you?" Salma asked.

"When she does, he beats her too. And if she asks him to just leave us and go live somewhere else, then he threatens us with an even worse beating," Rakan said, still not looking at her. "When I found you guys that night, I was running away from home, and I was *never* going back. I didn't mean to follow you guys. I just saw you by chance."

After a while, Rakan calmed down, the anger that had seized him fading away. It seemed like all he needed was to talk about things, in order for his anger to pass. It was another sign that he'd changed. He had started to trust other people a little. Now, he knew it was possible that there were people who would listen to him sympathetically, and maybe even help.

We went on for days. We stopped only for a little rest, to eat the pine nuts we found and even handfuls of grass, or to sleep. Finally, we reached the outskirts of a village. The whole place reeked with the smell of bodies rotting in the streets. The houses were destroyed, the olive groves were burned, and even the farm animals hadn't been spared in the fires sparked by the bombing. We stood in silence, just looking at the devastation all around us. Then we noticed a wisp of smoke rising from one of the houses. Salma walked up and touched one of the walls. She came back, saying, "The walls are still hot."

"So? What does that mean?" Rakan asked.

"It means the village was bombed only a few hours ago, and it's not safe here. Come on—we have to collect the stuff we're going to need before we go." She paused, then added, "I'll stay by the window, and one of you can look for a phone charger."

Rakan found a charger right away, near one of the wall sockets. We plugged in the phone and its light started to blink. I couldn't believe the electricity was still working in the middle of all this destruction! It was quiet in the house, and we rested a little, but before sunset the sound of bombing started up again, and I thought I heard bullets in the distance. I asked Rakan and Salma to get ready to leave the village immediately. We walked out through the kitchen door, and then we ran away at lightning speed.

We went a long way before stopping to catch our breath. "I think that house was a hideout for the gunmen," Salma said, still panting. "And they abandoned it after a new round of bombing,"

"I expect so," I said, before adding, "I was thinking the same thing a little while ago."

"What do we do now?" Rakan asked, sounding exhausted.

"We call our families," I said.

I switched on the phone, and before I could press the numbers to call my mother, Salma looked at me anxiously and asked, "Do you think they'll pick up?" I didn't say anything—I was just as worried as she was.

She watched me press my finger down on the call button. Then I was surprised by the dreaded voice: "Valued subscriber. This call cannot be completed due to an insufficient balance. Please recharge—" I threw down the phone before I could hear the rest of it, and I collapsed to the ground next to Rakan, disappointed.

Salma sighed as she picked the phone up off the ground and turned it over in her hands. Then she said, apologetically, "I forgot to buy more minutes."

Seconds later, the phone rang. Salma put it up to her ear and said, "Hello." Then she ran toward me, shouting excitedly, "It's your mother, Omar, it's your mother!" Before she put the phone in my hand, she added, "Thank God it can still receive calls."

Finally, Mama's voice came on, and oh God oh God, I'd missed her so much!

"Hello, Omar, my love . . . Say something . . . Hello, hello?"

My voice had died away, and I couldn't speak. Mama repeated, "Hello, hello, hello. Omar, Salma, Rakan, one of you—say something!"

It took everything I could to get control of myself and say, "Mama, I miss you." I heard her joyful sobs as she said, "Omar, my love, it's you! I couldn't believe it when I got a message telling me that Salma's phone was back in service."

My resistance broke, and I burst into tears as my mother went on speaking. "Don't cry, Omar. Alhamdulallah, thank God you're okay. Don't cry, my love. I'm fine, and Thoraya is too. We'll be together soon. I've been praying to God every day for us to be reunited."

I wiped at my tears and said in a strangled voice, "How are you, Mama?"

"Alhamdulillah, we're fine. Where are you now? How are you? How are Salma and Rakan?"

I turned it on speaker so that everyone could hear. Mama's voice was filled with hope, and she told us that everyone was doing okay, and that Salma's whole family, as well as Rakan's mother, were with her in the same camp near the border, a place called Ain al-Ghazal. Then she added, in a low voice, that Rakan's father had fled the bombing and they didn't know where he'd gone.

Mama asked us to search for a camp, or for one of the centers belonging to any of the relief organizations. They could get us to Ain al-Ghazal, she said. And she ended the call with a prayer that we all stay well.

# Chapter Twenty Three

We slept in safety, and in the morning we headed off down a dirt road. As long as there were cars using it, I guessed that it must go to *some* populated place—and we could see there were tire tracks in the dirt. At noon, we stopped at one of the stands of olive trees to rest a little. There, we found bullet casings scattered around, as well as traces of old campfires, empty food cans, and bags of garbage.

We noticed a bag hanging on a tree branch, and Rakan picked it up and started looking inside. Salma walked over and scavenged through the bag with him. Then she shouted, waving a doll in the air, "Omar, come quick!" I ran toward her as she said, "Look, this is Thoraya's doll! It was mine, and I gave it to her."

Before I even really understood what Salma was saying, I snatched the bag from her and started searching through it in confusion. I found the watch that Sufyan sometimes borrowed from me, and some of the clothes he used to wear.

"Sufyan was here," she said, with hope in her voice.

"Are you sure?" Rakan asked.

"Of course. We're close to him." I took in a deep breath, as if I could smell my brother's scent on the air. Then I added, feeling more confident, "I'm going to see him again. I will see Sufyan."

"But getting to him might be hard," Rakan said, lifting a dry stick to his mouth. "We might be putting ourselves in danger."

Without hesitation, I said, "It's up to you. As for me, I'm going to keep going, even if I have to do it alone."

"I didn't mean anything by that, Omar," Rakan said apologetically. "I'm not scared. But we just have to be careful."

Then came Salma's reassuring voice. "We're all staying together. We left together, we braved all this together, and we'll keep walking down this road together." She reached out a hand toward me, and I put mine in hers. Then Rakan pulled the stick out of his mouth and threw it down, walked over, and we all clasped hands.

I spent that night hugging the doll in my arms, as if I were hugging Sufyan. I couldn't sleep. Salma couldn't either, so she lit a small fire and sat next to me. She said, in a friendly tone, "Did you know that Sufyan didn't feel safe with you? To him, you were the weak and helpless brother."

"I know," I said, and it felt like a confession.

"But what you don't know," she said, "is that I *do* feel safe with you."

I looked over at her gentle face. Those were the sweetest words I had ever heard in my life. Maybe Sufyan was right, I thought. I hadn't been able to take responsibility. Maybe it was because I didn't have the courage to confront people. Then, after our father was martyred, I had sworn to change and to protect our family. I had tried my very best. But the war . . .

"So we'll be okay, even with the war breathing down our necks," Salma said, as I tried to hold back my tears.

We fell asleep just before dawn and woke to the sound of heavy gunfire. We decided to walk down a path that was a little off the dirt road, so that the gunmen wouldn't arrest us. After a while, we got to a hill that overlooked an ancient citadel. Despite the drizzle of rain, a haze of smoke and dust still rose up from the old building, surrounding it from all sides.

I almost couldn't breathe. Sufyan could be in there! With a glance at my expression, Salma read my thoughts.

"He's not in the citadel. He's fine. I prayed and prayed, and God loves me and listens to my prayers. Believe me."

Every time I heard Salma say this sort of thing, I felt calmer. I was sure that God loved her. God loves the good.

Carefully, we kept going, and after a while we heard voices nearby. We hid ourselves well. Then we saw a bunch of armored vehicles carrying men in black, heading toward the dirt road. Thank God we hadn't been walking on that road. Among the gunmen, I saw a man I recognized from the long scar on his face. He was the man who used to harass Baba, and who I'd seen once on TV. I tried to remember his name, but I couldn't dig it up out of my memory.

We heard the terrifying roar of warplanes heading toward the citadel, so we ran away as fast as we could. Then came the sound of explosions. We kept running with no thought of stopping or looking back. Where were we headed? We didn't worry about that part. All we worried about was making it out alive.

By noon, we'd run out of energy and couldn't keep going. We saw what looked like a cave entrance in a nearby wooded area in the forest. Salma hesitated before going in, maybe because she remembered that time with the snake. I gave her a look of encouragement. But since I was so tired, I couldn't say a single word.

Rakan went in first, and we dragged ourselves in after him. After a few steps, he stopped and said in a fierce voice, "Who's there? Hey. Who's there?"

I froze in place, waiting for Rakan to give me a signal, and so did Salma. Seconds of heavy silence passed before I heard the voice I'd been dreaming of for so long: "Who are you? Get out of here or I'll shoot!"

I cried out from the depths of my heart, "Sufyan! Sufyaaaan! Is that you?"

Then he appeared from out of the cave's darkness and ran toward me, throwing his arms open to hug me, and I did the same, and we were soaked in our tears of joy.

Sufyan introduced us to Ezzedine. Sufyan said he couldn't believe we were still alive, since the thugs from the Falcons of Truth had tricked him into thinking that we'd died in the bombing. I told him that Mama and Thoraya were fine, and Salma told him everything we'd been through. Sufyan listened carefully, but he wrapped himself in silence and opened his mouth only when necessary. Something in him had changed. It was as if he'd lost his sense of fun, and he was no longer the mischievous boy he used to be.

Ezzedine told me that the other boys who'd fled the citadel with them had been taken away in cars that all had the same logo on them, and he drew us the shape of that logo on the ground. After that, I knew we must be close to one of the centers for a relief organization. Together, we decided that the next step would be to get there.

The next morning, Salma suggested that we walk down the dirt road, and we agreed. A couple hours later, we saw an ambulance heading toward us, and we asked the driver to take us to the organization's center. He told us it wasn't far. And by noon, we were there. First, they did medical examinations of all of us. When they found the trace of drugs in Sufyan's bloodstream, they said he had to go in for treatment. We decided to stay there until he got better, and Salma started calling around, looking for Rayan.

During those weeks at the center, I clung to Sufyan as if he were part of me. I couldn't risk losing him again! He would wake up in the night, screaming, and then he'd clutch at me, begging me to help him get out of there. I would try my best to calm him down. I'd rock him back and forth, the way I used to do with Thoraya. Sometimes, I had to grit my teeth to bear his stormy emotions, which made him seem like a bird of prey stuck in a cage. Lots of times, I almost lost my cool when he would erupt like a volcano, screaming and crying, before returning to silence, sadness, and gloom. All I could do was to remind him of our old memories, the times we'd spent together.

It took a long time before Sufyan was cured. I remember that evening so clearly! After he took his medicine, he slept peacefully for the first time in months. And when he woke up in the morning, he was full of energy. He ate the rolled-up labneh and cucumber sandwich they gave us with real appetite, and then he asked if we'd go on a walk with him outside. I didn't hesitate for a second—I could feel the joy returning to his soul, the light in his eyes, the way his shoulders had relaxed. Salma joined us, wearing the dress that Umm Saeed had given her, her hair held back by a purple headband. A few minutes later, Rakan showed up too. We all sang Fairouz's "Kan Enna Tahoun" to celebrate Sufyan. Even though he didn't sing with us, I saw his face coming back to life.

I didn't ask Sufyan about whether he'd joined in the battles with the Falcons of Truth, or what else he'd done with them. I didn't need to hear whatever he might say. The scars on his hands and back, along with the trace of a long wound down his side, were enough to tell me everything.

Before the doctor decided that Sufyan had fully recovered, I sat with my brother out in the yard. He busied himself with whittling at a dry stick with a small knife, and I didn't know where he'd gotten the knife from. Without even noticing, he cut his finger. He didn't cry out, and he didn't seem to be in pain. He didn't even do anything to stop the blood that started to drip onto the ground. I told him it was time to for us to go to the camp where Mama and Thoraya were staying. He didn't show any excitement. Instead, he said he needed to stay here longer, and that he might not go anywhere. He said he had done things that God would never forgive him for. And then he started to cry.

I pulled him toward me and said, "We all make mistakes, but God always forgives us." Then I pointed up at the sky and added, "Look. If God didn't forgive us, then why would He make the sun rise for us every single day?"

Sufyan threw his head down on my shoulder and said, "I love you, Omar, my brother. I'm so, so sorry, and I'm begging you to forgive me." I hugged him tightly and said, "And I'm asking you to forgive me, my beloved brother."

The organization was able to make contact with Ezzedine's mother, and they brought him up to join her. Then Salma's efforts to find Rayan paid off; we discovered that he was getting treatment in a hospital, after his arm had been amputated because of gangrene. As for Ayham, he had started volunteering in a center for orphans. They were giving him an education, and he hoped to fulfill his dream of traveling around the world.

The whole way to the camp where our families had taken refuge, all I could see in my mind's eye was our little house in Raqqun. I closed my eyes to call up all its details, even silly things like our wall full of drawings of Spider-Man, and I imagined that I was playing out in the yard under the cedar trees, with my friends.

Outside, I noticed the signs of spring all around me. I loved this season. In the spring, the smell of pines hangs in the air, and the flowers I love bloom bright. I knew that, in the fields, the wild poppies had been burned away by war, just like everything else. But I remembered the story of Adonis. According to legend, whenever his blood was shed, these delicate red flowers sprang up.

It is hope . . .